Short, Short Fiction

To Read While

Pooping

An Eclectic Collection Of Fiction

For When Nature Calls

Volume I

by T.E. Whitmore

Trademark Disclaimer

Product names, logos, brands, URLs, web site links, and
other trademarks featured or referred to within this
publication or within any supplemental or related materials
are the property of their respective trademark holders.
These trademark holders are not affiliated with the author or
publisher and the trademark holders do not sponsor or
endorse our materials.

Copyright Acknowledgement

Legal Disclaimer

1.

Toothache

The voices were penetrating into his head like an oil derrick's drill penetrates granite. His mind fought, but ultimately yielded to the ever present buzzing cacophony of the voices. He was going mad and he knew it. Little time remained. Soon, there would be nothing left of his mind and all that would exist would be the warped thoughts they'd planted there.

He had to act. What could he do? He paced up and down the darkly lit room. It was noon. Fully daylight outside. But long ago he had covered the windows with foil in an effort to block out the voices. He couldn't let them win. He paced. He sweated. He was terrified. He felt like a condemned man at the gallows, waiting for the trap to open. He wanted more than anything to run away, stop his seemingly inevitable fate from playing, but he was impotent before the power of the voices. He knew of no way to shut them out.

He began to weep. He fell to his knees. Fear all but mastered him. He couldn't accept it. A fate worse than death. Life in a body not his own. Life in a body, a prisoner in his own mind forced to watch as a power not himself directed his flesh to acts he dared not imagine. He'd heard the voices. He heard them like he would hear screaming through a concrete wall. They were muffled. They were incoherent. He knew they were malevolent. Soon they'd be through and then they'd be in control. Soon the drill would break through his mind's resistance and that malevolence would pour in.

He had to act soon.

His tooth throbbed. It had been throbbing all day, increasing with the intensity of the muffled, malevolent voices. As they grew louder, more audible, the tooth hurt more. It was throbbing now, like a hot coal in his jaw. He'd been to the dentist recently. His tooth had hurt. He'd gone in to have it fixed. That's when the voices had started. Since then, those muffled, malevolent voices had grown larger and louder as the pain had increased slowly like the bass turned up on a stereo.

His mind snapped. It fired off in one final, ultimate, desperate act to stave off its own demise. He hadn't thought of it before. The dentist and the voices. The desperation and fear of the muffled malevolent voices had driven him to think of reality in ways he hadn't considered before. Could the dentist and those voices be connected? Was there some cabal between them and the dentist. The dentist had put something in him. She had opened the door to his mind for them with one of her implants. Something she had done had made it possible for those muffled, malevolent voices to find him, come to him and to grow louder.

It wasn't a lot to go on, but it was something. Desperate men do desperate things and cling to ideas easily. He had to try. He might lose. He might suffer a fate worse than death, but there was little to be lost now. If he did nothing, those malevolent, muffled voices would be through the stone walls of his mind soon enough. He was terrified. He was desperate.

He knew what he needed to do. He was out of options.

He fell to his knees. His heart was pounding. It was a mix. Fear of the voices and fear of what must be done drove the terror through his body. Pumping with a madness to match that of his tortured mind. His body was a fever pitch of activity as the valves of his mind snapped open and close and the valves of his heart followed suit. A contest between the two, like they were each straining their abilities to the breaking point in a contest to see which one would blow out first. Death or madness was coming. It was just a matter of which would occur first.

He had to act.

He screamed a primal scream. He reached into his mouth and grabbed the tooth. He held it between his thumb and forefinger with a dead man's grip. He screamed again. It was another primal scream. The neighbors were pounding now. The were terrified of the voice coming through their own walls. He pulled. He pulled with the strength and determination a condemned man uses against his shackles. He had nothing to lose.

His hands came loose and the dirty, metallic taste of blood filled his mouth. The blood ran, pouring out in rivulets onto the beige carpet. The voices went silent. The drilling stopped. He had thwarted them for now.

He'd won this battle, but he feared that the voices would return soon enough.

2.

At Least He Won't Sulk

What the fuck is he doing down there? Ouch! These boys and their nails. Get a manicure. That one hurt. Did he notice? Their so delicate, their egos I mean. If you aren't convulsing with waves of pleasure the second they touch you, then they go and sulk. Try getting fucked after that. Not gonna happen...

God, I just want to meet a man. A man who knows what he's doing down there and isn't just a little boy pretending, acting out what he's seen in porn. I don't mind a little bluster, but when it covers up the fact that you don't know what you're doing...ugggh. Again with the fingering. Guy, you don't need to do that. I feel like he's trying to poke a kidney. God, this guy is not good. Just bad. Do I give him the hook?

It started out like such a nice night. We went out. Met with a group of friends. Had some drinks. Had some laughs. We danced. He was cute. He seemed into me. It's been too long. Not since Jesse and I was beginning to think I didn't remember how. He started kissing me in the car. I kissed back. He let his hand slide over the side of my boob, like he thought he was sly. Like I didn't know what he was doing.

I thought "what the hell, I could do worse". I had a good buzz. I can always say I was drunk, that I didn't know better. But I had the itch, I was frisky and he was there. We came upstairs. We made out some more. Started on the couch, then lying on the couch. Clothes started coming off.

He had a nice chest. He kissed really well. Our tongues danced.

I stood up. I took his hand and led him to the bedroom. He tripped over some shoes I had on the floor. The room was a mess. I hadn't been expecting company, but I was a little drunk so I didn't worry about it. Drunk enough to now worry what he thought. I was excited. I was breathing hard. He was pretty good looking and it had been a really long time. Not since Jesse.

I took his shirt off. He got me topless, then my jeans came down too. Black panties. OK. Maybe I'd held out a little hope that someone might see them. He looked good with his shirt off, barefoot in those jeans. I was pretty drunk. I liked what I saw. He'd do. He'd do for tonight. I wasn't looking for Mr. Right. Just Mr. Tonight. I could always say I was drunk.

We made out some more. It felt good, his weight on top of me. Feeling that made me remember all that I'd been missing. I wanted more. I undid his pants and pushed them down. He wanted it too. That much was obvious. It pressed up against my black panties. I could feel it. Only those panties kept us apart. I ran my nails down his back, possessively. Mr. Tonight was mine.

He kissed down my tummy. He pulled of my panties. Lifted my legs up in the air. He took charge. Unwrapped me like a present. I wanted him. I was a little drunk. I held my breath waiting for him to take me. Then he went down. Unexpected. I wasn't ready. I hadn't shaved. Was I fresh? Fuck. He didn't stop, so I tensely held my breath, my body tight. He did his thing. He didn't do it well. Another man ruined by porn and a woman left wanting more. I mean, if you're going to do that, at least learn to do it right.

Damn. He really isn't good. Alright. A girl's gotta take charge sometime. Time to roll him over for a quick blowjob. At least he wont sulk then. I hope he's better at fucking.

He's still no Jesse. That's for sure.

3.

Dogs Can Run Faster

The first sign of trouble was the dog. He came running from the tall grass as fast as his muscular four legs could drive him forward. Dogs don't just run like that. Not in Africa.

I'd woken up that morning like any other and gone to work.

Life for a ranger on a game preserve is not much different than any other. You wake up and start your routine. Shower, breakfast and then you report for work. That day, there was a new batch of hunters coming in.

You may be shaking your head and looking down on people coming to Africa to hunt. But, the truth is hunting provides jobs, brings in money so my kids can have a better life and, at the end of the day, some species on the savannah need to be managed by humans. We've been here since the beginning and, as much as we'd all like to forget it, we're still part of the ecosystem. Herds needs to be culled to make them stronger and to ensure the survival of the species. We don't let them kill any elephants or rhinos or anything else that's endangered, but there are some species that are thriving in the modern era and those need to be attended to, even reduced. Here, we offer the chance for the wealthy to help us in that process for a fee. In many cases, an exorbitant one.

I got my assignment and went out to the reception area to meet the new batch of hunters. Mine was a baron. It's an outdated title that belongs more to the past than to the future, but mine insisted on calling himself that. He told me where he hailed from. Somewhere in Austria, Germany or Italy. For the former colonies, this sort of arrogance makes us bristle and I wouldn't dignify his pretentious airs by asking questions about his heraldry. I'll be honest. I didn't like the man from the beginning, but far be it from me to show anything but a large smile and warm hospitality. I do work in the service industry at the end of the day.

We made out preparations for the departure into the preserve the next day. The spotter plane that had brought in the guests had proceeded on to do some scouting over the preserve and we had good information as to where we could find plentiful game.

We rolled out of bed and left the compound before dawn. Animals like the heat even less than people do and when the African sun is at it's highest, they tend to lay low, hide somewhere and wait it out. The best hunting, like the best photography, is done early in the day, at sunrise, or late in the afternoon at twilight. I wanted, as much as the Baron did, to send him home with stories of great hunting and even better trophies. Happy, satisfied guests, come back, bring friends and money and prosperity for my community.

As we bounced across the unpaved road in out rover, the Baron and I talked, and I instructed him on the protocols of the hunt. We had a dog with us in the back who was to help us. Dogs in Africa are as useful as dogs in any other part of the world. More so even. A lion, a leopard, even a hippo can easily conceal themselves in the grass from a human and be on top of you before you know what's happening. The dogs, though, can smell the dangers long off and give ample warning. So as useful as they are in finding prey, they are doubly useful in finding the dangers.

I made sure to give the Baron the same speech I gave every client.

"The dogs can run faster than you can, so make sure you give them a good lead. Don't follow them too closely. They can turn around and bolt when they smell danger faster than you can. You'll need more time to react and more time to run from whatever spooked the dog than they will. Don't follow to close."

I can't tell you how many times I have made that speech. I know it by heart and I say it the same way every time.

Animals are unpredictable and sometimes, even the best information can turn out to be wrong. That's how the day went. The herds the plane had seen seemed to have vanished overnight and we had very few large animals, let alone any chances for a good kill. The dog flushed some game birds and the Baron had shot a few, but that wasn't why he had come to Africa. He'd come to shoot a springbok or a Cape Buffalo with the large, double barreled, antique rifle with the burled walnut stock he proudly and ostentatiously carried. It looked to be a hundred years old and for all I knew, Teddy Roosevelt could have used it when he was in Africa. But the game along the road and from the rover had proved disappointing and the baron had become frustrated, even irritated.

He kept asking to go off the roads, into the tall grass to look for bigger and better game. Anyone from Africa knows that that particular request comes with perils. You never know what lurks in the tall grass. I kept explaining it to him but he was more and more dismissive each time.

Finally, he became, abusive.

He broke into a tirade and began to curse me. Words that white men should never utter in Africa began to pour from his mouth as he accused us of cheating him, lying to him and taking advantage of him. It was all I could do to keep from striking him, but doing so, even under those circumstances would have cost me my job.

Ultimately, I told him, he could go into the grass, but I was not following and that I would wait where we were. All the same, I kept the engine running. He muttered something under his breath as we disappeared into the tall grass, taking the dog with him. I should have put up more of a protest, but I really did not like the baron.

The dog running, bolting really, from the grass was the first sign that anything was wrong.

I didn't have to guess at what was happening. Something the dog had sensed had spooked it and it'd run from fear. I silently hoped to myself that the Baron wasn't lion food already. I thought, as I threw the jeep into gear and sped the two hundred meters towards the dog, that I shouldn't have let him into the grass. It'd been a decision made in haste and anger, and those are so often wrong.

The ridge back was running towards me as I rolled over the dusty road and I slammed on the brakes to let it into the open top truck. It hopped without encouragement and meekly cowered in the back seat. My eyes met it's own scared pupils staring back at me.

As I looked back to where the dog had emerged, I saw the Baron himself burst from the grass, with a furious ostrich on his heels. As he came out, he immediately made a ninety degree turn and shook the monstrous bird from his tail for a second. They can run fast, but turn slowly. That little maneuver, intentional or otherwise, is probably what saved him from being disemboweled. Ostriches can easily end a man's life. It gave him enough time to run the few remaining meters to the relative safety of the jeep.

His face was that off a madman, wide eyed, mouth foaming in the few seconds it took for him to get into the open topped car. The frenzied ostrich was in no mood to give up the attack and kept up the attack as we sped away. It even followed for a time, easily keeping up with us until I was able to get into fourth gear. By then, we began to distance ourselves and eventually the prehistoric bird lost interest or gave up.

The Baron was a tad bloodied and bruised from the ordeal, but appeared to be largely unharmed, not counting his pride. As we rolled off it was hard to hide my smile at the foolish man's lessons in the perils of Southern Africa. He'd been lucky really. If he'd run into a lion when he ignored my professional advice, he most likely would not have returned from the grass..

"I dropped my gun." The baron said in a muted, shamed voice, not even looking up.

"It was my grandfather's."

It was hard to be sympathetic. Not long ago this man had called me a coward, among other reprehensible things, and had refused my very good advice to plunge headlong into the bush. He'd gotten what he deserved, a lesson, and in his fright he'd lost a family heirloom. It served him right as far as I was concerned.

"I think you followed the dog to closely.", was all I could get out before I began erupting with laughter.

4.

A Tryst

They were in the bathroom upstairs. They'd snuck away from work. Everyone thought they were on an errand. It was their dirty little secret. She was on the counter, legs spread, her skirt up over her knees. No panties covered the dark hair between her thighs. She was a hippie and proud of it.

He was tight laced with short hair. He was her boss. They were an odd couple as he stood there, between her legs kissing her with her arms wrapped around his neck pulling him into her embrace. There really is no explaining attraction.

Their kissing was steamy and hot. It was the kind of kissing you get when you aren't supposed to be kissing. It was the kind of kissing you get when you are cheating on someone. For them it was both. No one could find out about this. The bosses couldn't know. Their significant others couldn't know. Their coworkers couldn't know. That's what made it such a thrill. That's what made it such an alluring act - the risk. They had to hurry. If they were gone too long, they'd be missed.

Enough foreplay. He lifted her up onto her feet and spun her around. She bent over the counter, over the sink and threw her right leg over the counter. He needed no coaxing. The sight of the soft skin between her legs so prominently displayed was enough to send any man into overdrive and he'd been thinking of taking her to this bathroom for hours. He'd fantasized about it and now, here it was, in front of him.

He dropped his pants and threw his red tie, still knotted at the neck over his shoulder. He took the head of his throbbing member and rubbed the moist tip up and down her vulva, gently spreading the lips and leaving a slippery trail as he went. She inhaled, held it, and waited eagerly for him to plunge. She didn't wait long.

He pressed the full force of his hips into her and put all his weight behind it. She recoiled a bit as all of him slid into her, backed by the weight of his large muscular frame. She gasped and let out a little squeak of pleasure. He wanted her badly and was eager to prove it. He placed his hands on her hips. He grasped her tightly, possessively, like she was his and began to move in and out with intention.

She moaned. She'd been thinking of this too and the feeling of a cock other than her husband's was a thrill. It was a dirty thrill. She wasn't supposed to be here and she was excited to be breaking the rules. The thought of another man filling her made her tingle. This man was forbidden and this man was inside her. He moved his hand up to her shoulders and began pulling her back towards him, pushing deeper and harder into her. He was fucking like a man possessed and she wouldn't have stopped it for the world.

He was pumping and bucking rhythmically now. She knew he was building towards orgasm inside her. He was fucking with purpose. He was going to cum in her. He was going to claim her, if only for the moment. She pressed her hands into the counter to brace her body and looked at herself in the mirror. She smiled. She saw his reflection looking at her as she did so. He smiled too. Their eyes locked in the glass as they watched each other in this tawdry embrace. They felt it. They lived it. They watched it.

His hands tightened and he cried out. She watched his face bunch up as he released. She could feel it. He relaxed. He went limp and he pulled out of her. She could feel him, what he'd left run down her thigh as he did so. He pulled up his pants while she watched in the mirror, still bent over.

"Wait a few minutes. Clean up. I'll see you on the floor when you get back. That was great." He smiled and walked out of the bathroom, after a playful slap on her ass.

She looked at herself in the mirror and smiled too. The risk made it alluring.

5.

Walking 'Em In

Hassan sat in his old Japanese pickup. Like him, it had seen its share of wear and tear, but it still ran well. It was dark. Close to midnight and the lights of the city below put off an amber glow that made it hard to see the stars. They'd be here soon and then there'd be a show.

He'd gotten word from his handler a few days before. It had

gone on too long. The weapons were getting through and the depot needed to go. It couldn't be tolerated anymore. Lives were being lost and they could no longer turn a blind eye to it. He was to observe, to be the man on the ground to make sure the bombs fell were they needed to and that the target was destroyed. If there was a problem, if the bombs missed or went off course, he was to report it and wait for instructions.

The planes were already on the way. They were silent, invisible to radar and to the people on the ground, moving swiftly, effortlessly below the stars Hassan couldn't see.

It was getting close. He picked up the satellite phone he'd been given and dialed the number they'd given him. A man answered. No name.

"Hello" said the raspy voice.

Hassan repeated the numbers he'd been given and told the voice the color his handler had given him as verification. Aquamarine.

"Wait" was all the voice said.

Hassan's heart was pumping. A lot was at stake. People were going to die. Money was on the line too. He got paid for this work. He believed in what he did. His country was involved in things that brought trouble to the citizens. It brought hardship and he wanted it to stop. He wanted peace for his country. He wanted it to have a chance to get back on its feet. He wanted oil to be pumped and schools to be built for his daughters, but he did want the money too. That money would buy a better life for all of them in the here and now. If they found, him, especially when the bombs exploded, here, alone, with a sat phone, he would be lost. He was taking a risk and needed reward for the trouble, whatever his convictions.

The first explosion lit up the night sky like an orange sun at dawn. It was enormous. There were others, and secondary explosions from in the complex. Munitions exploding in a chain reaction. The steel roof of one of the hangers lifted off and flipped onto the parking lot below. Hassan's old truck rocked on it's axels in the aftermath and debris from the blast cracked the windshield. Hassan panicked. He threw the truck into reverse and slammed on the gas. The tires spun in the soft soil under him.

"Wait. Stop" the voice on the sat phone commanded.

He'd forgotten the open phone line.

Hassan said nothing as he looked over his shoulder and sped away from the blast.

"Stop! Now!" the voice roared. This time, a cold, menacing tone came over the line. Hassan complied. Far enough. He was safe. He tried to get his breath.

"The building on the North side. Is it gone?" the voice interrogated.

"Yes." Hassan choked out. "It's totally destroyed. No walls standing."

"Were there secondary explosions?"

"Yes. Many."

Sirens could be heard now. They were coming to put out the fires. Hassan could barely breathe from a mixture of panic and the acrid smoke in the air. He had to go. If the police found him, after the factory had exploded, with a sat phone, there was no telling what they'd do.

The words came.

"Thank you. We're good. Dismissed." came over the sat phone as the call clicked to an end.

He was done. They'd be in touch. These people were as

good as their word. The money would be forthcoming. He drove off into the smoke filled air as more, frequent and smaller explosions sounded out behind him. It was over – for now.

6.

A Hemingway Experience

They'd promised me tuna and a Hemingway experience. We'd covered thirty miles of churning ocean under the bright, burning tropical sun that morning.

The day had started calm, but the winds had kicked up. The water had turned rough and I'd learned just how significant a six foot swell was face to face. It was not nothing, like I had thought it was. At times I looked up at walls of water hanging precipitously above our rocking, little boat.

It had all started by me walking through grassy surf on a white sand Caribbean beach to reach the twenty foot open boat. It was pea green and the water was as rich a turquoise as I'd ever seen it. The day was beautiful. My guide was an ex-pat living down there to live the life all Americans dream of. He was bald, with perpetually red skin. Leathery, like the kind white men get when they live under a tropical sun that hates them. He was chatty and I think he was mostly talking to himself. I couldn't hear much over the roar of the forty horsepower motor that skipped our boat over the sea. But, I did hear snippets. He'd married a local. He had two kids in private school. He made his money showing vacationing dentists and tax attorneys a good time on the azure sea that was his backyard. He loved tuna and he didn't own a car. I would be lying if I said I didn't envy him. To me, he seemed free. He seemed genuinely calm, content and happy.

We started looking for fish by following the sea sparrows. The guide said that they were our best friends out here in the open water. They hunted the fish that the tuna hunted and they always seemed to know where the big fish were. I watched in amazement at the unending, energetic stream of small birds silhouetted against the bright sky. They seemed to skip like small black stones on a pond. They flew in small groups of twos and threes, whizzing low over the waves. They flew out from the land into ever deeper waters and we followed the stream as fast as our engine could go, dragging deep trawl lines in our wake. I was excited, expectant and eager.

Our boat flew through the waves, following the birds. The weather worsened. The strong wind began to rise from the east. The waves grew larger and the sea became turbulent.

The sky darkened. The boat rocked. Now and again, a wave crashed over the side and added to the reservoir of seawater already in the boat. My eyes kept nervously glancing down at the deepening pool. My leathery companion didn't seem to notice. His attitude offered me little comfort.

I could feel my heart start to beat harder. It was pumping now. I asked him how deep the water was. Three thousand feet. I looked around for life vests, for if we capsized. None were in the boat. They were unnecessary. This was a Hemingway experience after all. Man versus nature. I should have expected no safety precautions. I didn't say anything. I didn't want to be thought a coward, but I was nervous. My hand shook slightly.

Then, I saw it. A spectacle to say the least. Two old men, Indians, in their canoe, alone with us, atop three thousand feet of water in the middle of a very angry sea. They were standing. They were standing , perfectly balanced, in a canoe, like any you've ever seen at a summer camp lake, pulling in tuna with their hands and bare lines. They used no poles. They had none. They were calm and paid us no mind. They just worked their lines like they did every day. This was their livelihood. They were fishermen at peace. I was an agitated tourist looking on.

The sea was too rough for us, the risk too high. A drowned gringo is always bad for business. My guide decided to head in. I was overjoyed – silently. We caught no fish. A failure to some. We'd been out for four hours, but I'd gotten my Hemingway experience. I'd seen both old men and the sea.

7.

Is There Someone Else?

She stood there, motionless like she'd been hewn from marble. Her fists were clenched and her arms hung by her sides. Her body was tight and rigid, like she was girded for an attack. Her eyes, though, told a different story. Her eyes told of a conflict inside her and a fear of what lay ahead as they became glassy and slowly filled with tears. It was almost too late to turn back.

I asked her again.

"Is there someone else?"

She stood there still, eyes watering, biting her lip. I thought she might draw blood. I knew the answer in my heart before she answered.

I asked her again. This time, panic and fear had crept into my voice. I was terrified at what would come next.

"Is there someone else?"

"Yes!"

She screamed that terrible, lonely word with the mixed emotions and the bitter regret one utters when they break and confess to a terrible crime. It laid me low like a cannonball. I felt my knees buckle. My stomach churned in sudden convulsions and I swear to this day, the room spun. I couldn't support myself and I fell into one of the worn wooden chairs that surrounded the dining room table.

Time stood still and what seemed to be eons in my head passed in tiny microseconds in the real world. Her body had been prepared for an assault. Maybe she thought I would hit her when she confessed, but it was me that fell. Her one word had hit harder than any number of fists or blows ever could have.

At that exact moment her cell phone rang. The lighthearted, jubilant unwelcome, intruding tones pierced the somberness of the room and seemed an odd juxtaposition to what seemed the end of our mutual world. She took it from her coat pocket. She looked at it.

"Is it him?" I asked in a tone of sarcasm, anger and sorrow.

"Yes. I'm supposed to see him tonight."

She'd already planned all of this, I realized.

I didn't cry. That surprised me. I looked at this woman, the woman I loved and I felt nothing. Shock seemed to have numbed me. It was surreal and I was unfit to deal with it in any way. My apathy seemed to confuse her too. She hadn't expected this. Maybe she had hoped for something more, a fiery to show passion or desperate begging. Maybe she wanted that. All I could offer at that moment was stunned indifference. There was nothing more in me.

"I'm going to go." She said quietly, almost under her breath, avoiding eye contact.

She wanted out of that house. It had become a sad place with her one word and she wanted out. I didn't blame her. I didn't want to be there either. I didn't want to be anywhere then. At least she had somewhere to go. I didn't even think I could stand up from that chair, but I did.

"I'll walk you out."

I'm not proud of it. I walked her to the door to go be with another man. I didn't know what else to do. I still loved her. I still cared about her. I couldn't hit her. She wanted to go. I wasn't ready to beg. That would come later. I didn't know what to say.

"I'll be back tomorrow morning. You won't hurt yourself will you?"

Her eyes were wet again. She bit her lip. He pain in her was evident. Maybe she wanted to say more. There were so many things to say. Neither of us was ready to say them. Those too would come later.

"No. I won't. I'll see you tomorrow. I love you."

"OK. Bye."

She started the car, backed out the driveway and drove to meet him.

8.

The Viper Beneath

I wasn't drunk. He didn't know that. He didn't need to. He didn't want to. He wanted me drunk with my inhibitions shed on the dance floor. He didn't want me with my wits and reservations and worries about what others would think. He wanted me aroused, eager, and excited. I was, without the liquor.

It was my night. I didn't live there. No one knew me. No one would remember me or what I did. I left my bashfulness in the hotel room when I went out. That night I lived only in the moment.

A single girl, attractive, I dare say, gains attention easily. Men notice. They're hunters and a single antelope alone on the plains is an easy target for a lion. They thought I was easy prey, but I was actually the hunter. I sat, in my skimpy, low cut dress, showing off all that I had. I looked the part of the flower, but my heart was that of the viper beneath. I waited, patiently for my prey to approach. He, whoever he was, had something I wanted and I was going to have it – on my terms. The damsel, seduced by the rogue.

A few approached me. These were fish not worthy of taking. Too young. Not enough panache. I was looking for a man who knew what he wanted. A stereotype to fulfill a long held fantasy.I wanted him to think that he was taking me, even though, unlike a lady, I was taking him. I sat, drinking my virgin Cape Cods and busied myself looking helpless.

Finally, the lion I sought approached me. We talked. I laughed. He laughed. I sucked down more virgin drinks. I spilled one and looked clumsy. We danced. He thought I was drunk and let his hands wander more than a lady should let a gentleman. I let him. His hands stirred me. He got closer. I could feel his breath on my neck.

He took my hand and led me. Towards the bathrooms. I knew what he was doing. I knew what I wanted and what I sought that night was in the bathrooms. I followed. He opened the door and led me in. The door locked behind us. I giggled, feigning drunk – seeing the act through to the end.

The bathroom was filthy, but that's what I wanted. I wanted filth. I wanted to feel cheap and dirty and I wanted a stranger that nigh. Everything I needed was locked in the room with me.

He pressed me to the wall. I could feel his body weight pin me. We kissed. He lifted my leg and ran his hand between my thighs. I could feel his cock as he pressed into me. He was no gentleman but he knew what he wanted and he was going to take it. I wanted it too. I wanted to be taken.

He pulled down my panties and lifted my short dress over my hips. I turned and presented myself. His aggression had won what he sought. Bent over a sink in a stinking bar bathroom, I heard him unzip. I heard his belt buckle jingle as his pants fell to his ankles. He entered me roughly, without thought. Only urge drove him. His right hand pulled back on my shoulders as he fucked me. His left was on my hip. I braced myself so my face wasn't pushed into the mirror. He pumped. He grunted and cried out as he released, his face twisted amusingly. I was sober, but he was tipsy and brief.

He panted and held still for a minute. My heart raced. Exhilarated. I told him I'd meet him back in the bar. I lied. I slipped out the back. I was done with him and discarded him. In my heart, I hoped he'd forever wonder what he'd done wrong.

9.

Guard Duty

Moshe hated guard duty. It wasn't that he was afraid of dying, he was just afraid of being killed. He'd heard enough stories at the kibbutz dining hall and in the fields of what the fedayeen could, would and had done to wire guards at other kibbutzim. It was lonely too. Not enough people for the whole perimeter. They were always promised Haganah men from Tel-Aviv, but they never came. They were needed elsewhere.

Moshe understood, but that didn't bring him any comfort. It was just him, under a moonless starry, night against the hordes of enemy soldiers he imagined waiting to kill him out there in the inky, cold blackness. Plus Moshe really had to pee. Tea always ran through him but he needed the tea to stay awake. Moshe always found it hard to get the water flowing when it was this cold anyway. He just held it and hoped it would help to keep him awake for when the fedayeen attacked.

Moshe woke with a start and a panic. Where was he? What was that noise? For just a split second, he looked around and couldn't remember where he was. Why wasn't he in his bed? Then he remembered. Guard duty. The war. The fedayeen. The quest for a homeland after all that had been taken. His hands naturally gripped the warm, worn, wooden stock of his old Belgian Mauser. It was a reflex. The fear was coming back and the old rifle with only three bullets in the magazine was his only small comfort.

He'd drifted off to sleep, but the noise that'd woken him had caused his heart to beat violently and his hands to shake. Sleep wouldn't come easily now. He was wide awake.

There it was again. Someone stepping on the rocks. Fedayeen creeping up to his position to lob a grenade into his fighting hole. They were getting closer. He could hear them. He could hear them coming to rampage through the kibbutz. He scanned desperately, looking for them. He squinted but could see nothing. But he knew they were out there. He could feel a rifle sight trained on him. Fear coursed through Moshe's body as his muscles tightened.

His trembling fingers clicked off the safety of his old rifle. He braced the the old gun against his shoulder, slowly so they wouldn't see him. His heart pounded. It was like thunder. He wondered if they could see him. He knew he couldn't run and hide, as much as he wanted to.

He lined up the sights. They were hard to see in the dark. He squinted. He scanned again looking for anything that could tell him where the marauders were. Then- a sound. Footsteps on the rocks again. He swung the rifle to point at the noise and he fired without thinking or aiming. A flash from the muzzle cracked the darkness and the report of the rifle thundered across the valley.

The alarm went up. The kibbutz sprang to life like an anthill tipped over. Men and women ran to the perimeter and to Moshe. He wasn't alone now. There was safety in numbers.

"What was it?" a faceless young man asked.

"Men in the dark." Moshe replied. Then silence. They waited for the attack. Nothing happened.

Ari, the oldest at nineteen, went out to look, silently creeping forward, bravely, into the dark. Nothing. Then they all heard laughter.

"Bring a lantern!" Ari roared out, as he chuckled.

Moshe did as he was told. A hundred yards out, Moshe found Ari, with a dead goat at his feet.

Ari looked him in the eyes, "You did good kid. I'm pretty sure it's an enemy goat. Help me get it to the kitchens. Shouldn't go to waste."; still laughing and shaking his head.

"At least you'll stand your ground. You did real good."

10.

Aventura Sur Al La Frontera

No one who has ever used the urinal in a Mexican cantina would blame me for opting to stagger out and piss on the wall of the bar instead. I did. Who could blame me? They're disgusting. Yes I was drunk, but that didn't take away from my ability to be sickened by the assaulting smell

41

of ammonia in there.

So I staggered outside looking for a wall to paint in my own style. I found one. It was brick, and bordered on a dark alley that seemed to extend forever. The street lights hurt my eyes after hours spent in the dark, loud bar, so I rested my face in the crotch of my arm, held my beer loosely in one hand and blindly aimed my member with the other. Up til then, it'd been an amazing trip. Lots of fun under a bright Mexican sun.

A man's in his own bubble when he's peeing. Men's rooms are quite places. No one talks. Maybe a newspaper rustles, but that's it. I was in my bubble, in my own world, enjoying the pleasure of release when a hand gripped onto my right shoulder. Panic set in. I was under attack I thought. I spun around, still peeing, peeing on myself in the process, all over my shorts, to find two Mexican policia staring at me shaking their heads slowly from side to side.

Police were worse than getting robbed.

"You. You're under arrest." One of them said in perfect English touched with a northern Mexican accent.

"You're coming with us." The other said. His accent was much thicker and he was harder to understand.

I didn't know what to say. I was stunned. I was panicking. My heart was about to burst out of my chest. If I hadn't just pissed all over myself I would have then.

"Fuck" was all I could stammer.

One of them took me by the arm, the other on the opposite side. They began to walk me to the station. Arrested in Mexico. This was not good. All the rumors I'd ever heard about Mexican jails flooded into my mind. Fetid water to drink. Nothing to eat. Assaults. Poop buckets. My mind was swimming and my hands began to shake anxiously and noticeably.

We walked and then suddenly the man holding my arm steered me towards another, different darker alley extending to nowhere. My mind exploded. Nothing good was down that alley and all I could think about was my head, severed, in a disposable ice chest on the side of a deserted highway, festering in the Southern heat.

I could not go down that alley. Nothing good was down that alley.

"Woah. Woah. Why are we going down this alley?" I ejaculated.

"No. Look. Here. Take all my money. Take it!" I stammered as both my hands desperately reached in and began to pull out all the money in my pockets.

I threw it on the dusty ground. All of it. I held back nothing. Hundreds of American dollars and even more colorful Mexican pesos lay in the dirty road. The cops looked at each other. Looked at me and nodded. OK. I could go.

I ran. I ran, and I'm not one who runs, like I would have with a puma at my heels. I found my friends. I told them the story.

"Fuck. I need another beer.", was all I could say at the end.

I borrowed a few pesos from a buddy and tipped back another ice cold, Mexican lager.

Robbed in Mexico is still better than arrested in Mexico.

11.

A Window In San Fran

A red eye out of SFO was waiting for Sadie. She was supposed to fly out at 5:30 the next morning. She was stuck in her hotel room. She needed to sleep, but just like anytime she needed to, she couldn't. She was wired.

It'd been a commando raid of a business trip. Flight one day, presentation the next and she was supposed to leave at 5:30 AM the next morning. All in all, she'd been in San Francisco for 36 hours – maybe. She was exhausted. Her body craved sleep, but her mind would have none of it. She looked at the clock. With it's red LED numbers, it spelled out 9:30. She sighed. 9:30 PM was way too early to go to bed anyway. She thought to herself that she shouldn't have even tried. She was frustrated. She was expected back in the office in Vancouver tomorrow and she knew she was going to be a zombie.

She paced.

Sadie looked out the window of her hotel room. It was an old hotel. It had been built right after the 1906 earthquake. It had charm. It was Victorian elegance and you couldn't beat the location. She stayed there every time she went to the Bay Area. She'd looked out these windows overlooking the courtyard of the hotel many times. She did it to see the view, maybe to see the sky, but now and again, secretly, she hoped someone had left their window open accidentally. It was a sinful desire, one she'd barely admit to herself and certainly to no one else. If her boyfriend had been there, she wouldn't have done it. To him, she was a lady. But he wasn't there so, she scanned like a pervert.

She sighed.

All the windows were dark, or the curtains were drawn.

Just as she was about to turn away and go lie back in bed for more restless not sleeping, one of the windows lit up. The lonely light had the same drawing effect as a lighthouse during a storm. She peered intently.

There was nothing at first. Just a lit up hotel room that looked much like her own. Then they came into the area that Sadie could see. They were attractive. Both looked like they were in their 30's. The were dressed elegantly in formal wear. Sadie assumed they were guests from the hotels banquet room. They must have come from a wedding. Maybe they were in the wedding party, sneaking away for a rendezvous.

Then, Sadie's eyes grew wide. The two embraced, and began to kiss and undress one another in a flurry of passion. The way the clothes came off, it was clear to Sadie that the dam that held back the desires of these two had just burst. Now the river was free to run its course.

She wasn't supposed to see this. She knew it. She was seeing something exotic and forbidden. A rarity. It was like catching a glimpse of a white rhino on safari. You have to look. To not look would be an insult. She loved it. She watched. She stared. She didn't blink. She didn't want to miss anything.

The scene across the courtyard was torrid. It was passionate. It was even acrobatic. The two women across the way put on a show. They contorted, caressed, sucked, licked, tickled and cooed. Sadie was excited. She wished her boyfriend was there after all.

Then a start. One of them, the woman, got up from the embrace and walked to the window to close the curtains. Sadie held her breath and was motionless. She didn't want to be seen, but she stared all the same. Then, the woman across the way waved. Eeeps! She waved at Sadie. Panic! Sadie darted behind the curtains and jumped under the covers.

The rest of the sleepless night, Sadie waited for the knock of the hotel manager on her door. None came.

12.

People Skills

It was a beautiful house. Cedar shingles covered the sides of it and it lay nestled in its own isolated cove along the rocky Pacific coast. It was picturesque, isolated and a private retreat. It was a moonless night and the sky hung, jet black, save for the explosion of countless stars normally drowned out by the city lights.

She was in the house. He was driving up the rocky driveway throwing up dust as he went. Neither of them knew I was watching from the stand of tall firs next to the driveway. I was prostrate, covered in black and I had been watching for a week. I knew them well by now. As he reached the end of the driveway, I rose slowly to my knees and prepared.

The silver German car came to a halt and the persistent glare of the red tail lights leaked into the blackness. He always kept his foot on the brakes when he was in the driveway. I had seen this before. By then, I was standing. There was little chance of being seen. I took the safety off the shotgun and quietly chambered a round. The persistent roar of the waves covered the noise.

He opened the door and I began my approach. Slowly, cautiously, weapon raised, ready to shoot. I had planned it all in my head before. I was ready. This wasn't my first time. As I moved and breathed, my hot breath was caught in the ski mask and began to radiate a hot, wet heat over my face.

He never did see me coming.

I whistled. He spun around revealing his chest and I fired. He was down on the first shot. Sure enough, just as I had expected, she came running out of the house to see what the commotion was. People always run to gunfire. I'd seen that before too. It's weird. By then, I had chambered another round. By the time she saw me, I was already firing. She was down in one shot too.

Now don't go and I think I am some kind of cruel assassin. I'm not. I use rubber shotgun rounds. They hurt. In fact, they incapacitate when you take one in the guts. You will drop, stunned, even with body armor. But they won't kill you. Technically, they're called "less lethal". I suppose they can kill, but they never have with me. They just drop you and make you more manageable.

She was lying on the front porch, he was lying a few yards

in front of me coughing, trying to catch his breath. Both had broken ribs. I was pretty sure of that. I walked up to him first. I took out the zip ties in my vest and laced him up fast. A canvas bag over the head. I ran over to her. I moved her hands behind her back. She offered no resistance. Manageable. Hands bound, bag over the head. I dragged them both against the side of the house and sat them up.

I explained to them in no uncertain terms what was happening. I was there for the marijuana. It was mine and they were going to wait patiently while I took it. I told them both, that if they resisted, we would rape her, before we killed them both. There was no we. I was alone. No one was raping anyone. I'm a thief, not a monster. It was just business. A job. But a little terror inspires cooperation. Pot farmers are usually compliant, but terror ensures it.

"Please...please...please..."

They were both pleading for their lives over the persistent sobbing, gasping and praying. They begged me to take what I wanted and just leave. Efficient. Diplomatic. Proficient. And my guidance counselor said I had no people skills. What did he know?

13.

Mr. Orson

Mr. Orson closed the door of the bathroom. He locked it, instinctively. There was no need. No one would bother him. He was alone in the old house. He'd been alone for a long time. He was old in the old house and he was alone. Outside, the rain and the cold wind pattered against the single pane of the bathroom window. He paid it no mind. He plugged in the space heater he had just bought. He turned it on to full blast. He was old. He was cold. For once, he could do something about that. No need to be uncomfortable.

It had been a long day. Winter had started and the day was short and dark. He had arisen before sunrise and cooked breakfast, alone, like he always did. He sat at the small table he and his wife used to share and he ate in the silent house. Most days he turned on the TV and the voices took the edge of the stillness, this morning, he had embraced it. He had eaten quickly. He had a lot to do.

As he left the house, he fiddled with the ring in his pocket. He knew what it looked like. He had bought it a long time ago and had seen it on Anne's finger every day of their marriage. When the cancer finally took her the pain had been too much and she died without it on her finger, in the hospital. The ring was in the box at home, safe. He had kept it as a precious memento, but today, it was a tool. He needed it. He needed the money it would bring and he took it to the pawnbroker.

He didn't haggle much. Pawnbrokers are shrewd men and he only needed so much. Mr. Orson got him to that price and they struck their bargain. He had enough – for a while. He walked out of the pawn shop to the ring of the bell on the door, thanking the man for giving him enough. It wasn't his only stop and he was in a hurry. He needed other things.

He went to the bank. They had been after him. He had fallen behind in the payments and they were talking about taking the house. It should have been paid off, but Anne's cancer had been expensive. He met with a banker. He eased into the black leather chair in front of his desk. It hurt. His bones were stiff and it was cold in the bank. It was always cold in the bank. He didn't talk much. He laid the cash from the ring on the banker's desk. He applied it to his mortgage, brought it current, with enough for three months after that. It was enough time. He could breathe easily for a bit. The banker tried to sell him some new products. Mr. Orson wasn't interested. He had enough already.

He went to the store. It was his last stop. It might not seem like a lot of errands but to an old man, with cold, sore bones, it was a lot of work. It was much more than he ever did on normal days. He was making the effort. He had to hurry and it took all he had to keep going. He bought what he needed and went home. He took his bags and went into the bathroom and locked the door.

He plugged the heater in first, then sat on the toilet and caught his breath. He wasn't done yet. There was more to do.

He rose and pulled back the blinds. He took out the caulk and the gun and began to seal the wood frame windows. His hands weren't steady, but could hold them still enough to lay a good, straight line of caulk. When he was done with the window, he turned to the door. There was enough caulk. The room smelled of chemicals when he was done, but he was happy with the work. It was a good seal. The heater had made the room as hot as the summer he spent in Miami with Anne and his mind wandered over happier times for a minute.

He sat on the toilet, placed the revolver his dad had left him in his mouth and pulled the trigger. Just before the hammer clicked, he thought of Anne one more time and smiled at the thought he'd be with her soon.

What was left of Mr. Orson sat on the toilet in the empty, still house. Only the hum of the heater broke the silence. He'd sit there, in that room, in that hot room, until the sheriff's came to foreclose on the empty house, just like the bank had been threatening for months. They hadn't listened and he was too tired to fight anymore.

By then, time and the heat would have done their work. They'd find what was left of Mr. Orson in that still, empty, ruined house. No one would bother him until then. No one would know, the caulk seal would see to it that the house kept it's secret until they foreclosed.

They could have the house then. He was done with it.

14.

Warm Amber

The light in the room was soft, warm and comforting. It bathed the suite in an amber glow that mesmerized and comforted simultaneously.

The day had started like any other. Get home from work, drink a bourbon, unwind, relax. She had called me late. Well after dinner. It had been short. She wanted to come over. She wanted to see me. I didn't get to see her all that often so I agreed.

It had been even later when she arrived. Almost too late. She had pulled up in her flashy car and opened the door with her key. She was practically at home. She poured herself a drink at the bar. I helped myself to another. Conversation had been been light. Trivial. Fleeting. It was a nod to appearances, nothing more. Karen was there to play with one of her toys. I would've been offended if I didn't like being played with so much.

Her visits were always a pleasure. She blew in like an arrogant, sweet, soft summer breeze on chilly nights. She'd have a drink, we'd chat idly, briefly, and then get down to it. We didn't have much time. Rushed lovemaking is not bad lovemaking by any means. In some cases, it makes it better. The rush makes you focus, think carefully amid a flurry of twisting sweaty flesh and heaving breaths. You fuck with purpose, intention, concisely. A little oral, a little cowgirl or doggy. Everyone has a good time. Everyone has fun. Everyone gets their fortune cookie.

We laid there after the act bathed in that warm, soft amber light. Karen's skin always looked fantastic in that light. It smoothed everything out and gave warm bodies a dreamlike quality, like pictures in a magazine slightly out of focus. It was our indoor silent veil and it made the room and the people in it dimly beautiful.

She lay there, sidled up to me. My arm was around her. Her dark hair flowing over her back and onto the pillow she lay on, my arm bathing in the cascade. Her body was warm. She was sweaty and sticky when I traced my finger over her skin. So was I. Her hand was on my tummy slowly moving in small circles while I smoked a cigarette and watched the amber blue smoke melt into the warm light. She didn't say anything. I didn't either. It had all been said before. Nothing had changed. Nothing was going to change. We just lay in dim beauty, each of us in our own heads next to a pleasing warm body.

The time came that I hated. She had to go. Out of our warm dream, back to cold reality. It came every time. I knew it would. So did she. We never talked about it but both of us thought about it. I did at least. I wonder if she did too.

She lifted her curved body off the bed and walked across the room into the bathroom. This was always my favorite part. She never covered herself but walked through the room like she owned it, proud as a queen while my eyes poured over her milky white flesh. A Botticelli in real life, bathed in a dim, warm amber light. I'd seen it before, but each time I looked at her as she crossed that room was like my first. I savored it every time.

She turned on the light in the bathroom and the silent warm veil vanished with a flood of cold fluorescent light. That was the sign. The dreamer was awake and reality had won out. That was it. It was over. Back to life.

Me back to my bourbon, Karen back to her husband.

15.

Submission

Juan was on his knees, with his forehead to the floor. His wrists burned where the handcuffs were cutting his flesh raw. They were tight. They were tight on purpose to heighten his discomfort. He was bathed in a white light from above, which formed a circle on the floor, in the dark, cold room.

His skin was clammy. He was nude. Sweat from the lights

quickly evaporated and gave his skin the feeling as though he'd been dead for an hour. His balls hung limply between his legs just barely above the floor. His eyes were covered with a stained, dirty rag and he couldn't make a sound due to the chewed piece of wood held in his mouth with a strap.

He couldn't get up. He couldn't see. He couldn't call out. He was helpless. He was at their mercy as they sat casually smoking a cigarette. The smell of the tobacco and the smoke hung in the air.

He lay there. He lay there waiting for what would come next.

He didn't have long to wait.

The blow fell across his back sharply like a gunshot. It cracked and pain seared through his body. His whole frame ached as muscles twitched from the explosion the nerves of his back telegraphed to every cell in his body. His spine contorted trying vainly to protect itself. His shoulders flexed automatically trying to free his arms to protect the body from more blows. They all failed. All they accomplished was to pull already raw skin against the unyielding strength of the cold, steel handcuffs. His spine straightened as it lost strength and his body fell limp again.

Still on his knees, with his forehead against the grimy floor.

Juan lay there drawing in quick, short, gasping breaths over the pain.

Another blow. Pain exploding across his body again. They were yelling at him now. Cursing him. Hurling a barrage of vile obscenities at him as the blows fell. His body reeled, the violence of the scene fell into a din and his mind turned in on itself trying to make sense of the attack. Trying vainly to block out the pain and the degradation. It tried anything it could like a fish trying to wriggle free from an angler's grip. It was strong and quick, but it failed again. The pain and the degradation were getting in, seeping into the mind and it was forced to accept the humiliation. It had to accept that it could not stop what was happening. It could only endure.

The blows didn't stop. They fell faster and harder and the obscenities became more vile and abrasive. Cunt. Bitch. Cocksucker. They fell like blows to his ego as his body alike. He was impotent to stop either but he struggled. His wrists were cut now. Raw. Bleeding. The blood flowed freely and he could feel the sticky blood dripping down his back onto the floor. It was bleeding now too.

They grabbed his head, lifted it up and yelled at him. He could feel hot breath. The words were directed right into his face, but he was disoriented. Blind. Mute. He was awash in pain. Their hateful words sounded to him as though they were being shouted to him through a pillow over his face. They were loathsome but unintelligible. All he could feel was the pain and his insignificance at the hands of his assaulter.

Juan reflected to himself amid the din of his muffled screams, their obscene utterances and the sound of blows falling on his own, beaten back.

Christine had been right. She knew her man. She had suggested a domination session for his birthday. He had always been curious. It was her gift to him and it was better than Juan had hoped.

16.

Hippias

The tyrant himself pressed the white hot brand into the soft flesh of her flank. It sizzled like bacon and the air hung thick with the oily smoke of burnt flesh and hair. She screamed. He smiled.

Her husband lay across the room on the limestone floor of the chamber. Dead. Putrefying. He was dead by his own hand and vengeance had been denied the tyrant. The husband had tried, vainly to unseat the tyrant and had run, like a coward, to death to escape the fate of all failed assassins. His end had been far to pleasant.

When the tyrant had learned of this, his mind had snapped into madness. Vengeance had been denied him by a cowardly act, but that did not mean his rage had been sated. Someone had needed to suffer for this crime. Someone had to present the outlet for the rage. Only once the rage had been vented would life be able to go on as it had before.

She screamed again as he thought, introspectively and pushed the brand against fresh virgin skin once more. It was a wail. A primeval wail that begged for a release from the pain that the mortal flesh was feeling. No relief was given. The tyrant would have his way and this woman would suffer. He placed the brand back into the iron brazier that held the coals. Its heat had been drained. Its ability to give pain was lessened and it would need to rest. It would have a long night.

For now, the tyrant would have to settle for cold steel. He picked up one of the knives on the stained wooden table.

He walked over to the woman as she panted, unable to speak, her tongue was gone and she swung limply back and forth from the chains that suspended her from the ceiling. Her eyes flashed. They darted around the room. They looked at her husband's mouldering corpse. They looked at the tyrant. They darted vainly in the hope of some deliverance from this chamber. They were desperate. They were desperate to escape what was coming.

The tyrant grasped a tuft of her hair, hard, with this left hand and pulled her head to the side. She screamed again, gagging almost, unable to breathe choking on blood and saliva. He wanted this. Her pain offered him the outlet to the rage that needed satisfying. He slowly began sawing through the cartilage of her left ear. He took his time and could feel the dull edge of the knife blade methodically work through. The scream had turned into one, unending, gasping cry that filled the chamber more than the oily smoke still hanging in the air. He tuned it out. He heard nothing as the ear separated and he threw it over his shoulder. He had only been interested in it when it was part of her and was an avenue to cause suffering. Now that it was separated it was another lump of rotting flesh and should be treated accordingly. He threw it over his shoulder onto the limestone floor with the other bits and pieces that'd accumulated. He never took his white hot mad eyes off of her. He was enjoying his playtime. His blood was up and he was nowhere near finished.

He walked back a few steps and sat down on the small wooden stool in the room. A cruel king on his favorite throne. He sat there and looked at the woman. He studied her like an artist studies a block of marble, considering his options. He considered how he wanted this piece to finish. What was he looking for? Suffering. Yes, but how best to do that? She hung there, her terror filled eyes darting about the room, her faculties failing her. It was nowhere near over.

17.

The Baby's Head

I'd sent her in to clean the men's room simply because I hated her and wanted to make her unhappy. She was that kind of employee. Annoying and you just wished she'd quit, but she hung in there. It made me understand how that damn coyote felt. No matter what you did that stupid bird got up with that stupid noise it made and then it would run off. That was her. My stupid, impossible to kill running bird. If I couldn't make her quit, at least I would make her scrub men's room toilets.

She went in there with a smile. Fuck her. Fuck her and that stupid smile. She was too stupid to know that I was being mean to her. I just shook my head and went back to my office.

She came back out almost immediately. She just barged into my office without so much as a knock.

"I can't do the bathrooms!"

"One of the toilets is clogged!"

I shook my head slowly from side to side. Can't even clear a toilet clog. Annoying and now worthless too. I'd seen this before. Time to lead from the front, or at least closer to it. I knew then that I'd have to take her in there and coach her about how to clear a toilet clog. I grabbed the plunger from its trusty box in the broom closet. Irritatedly, I pushed it into her protesting hands.

"It won't work. Trust me."

She was almost pleading now.

I scoffed at this. We went in the bathroom together, a look of fear in her eyes and I popped into the stall to scope out the situation.

My mouth fell open. People say that as a cliché, but it happens when you're truly shocked and I was shocked.

In the bottom of the bowl was a turd the size of a baby's head. I don't mean it was long like a baby, I mean it was as wide as a baby. No joke. Eight centimeters at least. It blocked the hole at the bottom of the toilet like a plug. I stepped back. I looked at her. She looked at me and she ran from the room. The door closed behind her.

A fucking coward. Annoying and worthless to the end. If the communists had been in power, they would have put her kind against a wall first thing. It would have been a good start. They just get in the way of people and progress.

She wasn't needed now. She wasn't up to this anyway. I knew this was going to take more than she had to offer.

I looked around for the dead man who must have given birth to this monster and then expired. None was there. I was surprised. There should have been someone. This monstrosity should have split him open. We should have heard the screaming. But there had been only silence before. A perplexing mystery that I would have to be solve later. I shook my head. This was nothing I had seen. It was like a three minute mile. It didn't happen. But there it was, plugging the hole in my toilet proudly defying to go into oblivion.

You had to admire it. It was the twenty pound lobster that had to be boiled, but you felt bad for it. It's sheer size commanded respect. But its size changed nothing, it had to be boiled.

I hesitated. I flushed. It resisted. It defiantly plugged the hole. It took it. My first assault had been repulsed. Something special was required. A regroup. This one wasn't going to go quietly. It had more fight than others.

I stepped back. I rubbed my chin pensively staring at my adversary. To defeat it, I had to be smarter than it. I had to out think it.

I walked across the tiled floor and opened the door. I yelled.

"Phil! Go outside and get me a stick. Oh! Get the camera from my office too. No one'll believe this otherwise."

18.

Andean Snowstorm

Jim had come to Peru to see the beautiful landscapes. He loved the high mountain peaks and the views. Machu Picchu had been more than he could imagine. How the Incas had built that lost city in the skies was beyond him. But, Jim had come to Peru for another reason. He would have been lying if he told you it wasn't on his mind. He'd come for the cocaine.

Jim was a traveler. He explored the world with a seventy five liter backpack strapped to his robust frame. When he'd explored Costa Rica all the other traveler's had told him to explore Panama. He had. When he was in Panama, all the people on the tourist trail told him about cocaine and ruins in Peru and Colombia. He figured, he had to see those too. He would have regretted it if he hadn't when he was old and gray. So he kept heading South and eventually made it to Lima.

The owner of the dingy hostel had been more than happy to help him out. Besides, it helped with the altitude sickness. People came to Peru for cocaine and the hotelier made his money catering to those people's wants and wishes. He'd been more than happy to help Jim find what he sought. It was pure white, like the snow on the high peaks.

There was a knock at the door. Lydia, the British ex-pat temporarily living in the room next door was knocking. Jim had invited her to savor the South American delicacy he had in front of him. He'd popped his head in (they knew each other casually by now) and had asked her if she wanted to partake. She said "she'd love a 'lil bump" and that she'd be over in a minute. She knocked just as Jim was finished laying out two lines on the night stands with the playing cards he always carried for airport layovers.

He told her it was open and she came in and sat next to Jim on the bed in a familiar manner. He offered her the first line, but she declined. Jim thought she was probably a little intimidated. This wasn't the blow they had done in college, this was the real thing – pure, uncut and powerful. Jim did the first line.

The sensation was instant, overpowering and reality became a blur.

The wobbling ceiling fan was the first object that came back into clarity. He was dazed. Jim's head hurt and he couldn't remember where he was. Then it came back. Peru. Thin air, high mountains and killer cocaine – apparently. His head was pounding now. He wondered what time it was. It was dark in the room. He wondered what time it was and how long he'd been insensible. The only light was the neon light of the hostel sign coming in through the closed drapes on the second story window.

Then, he heard a toilet flush and running water in the bathroom.

"Who's in my bathroom?" Jim thought to himself. He couldn't remember anything.

The door opened and the light from the bathroom flooded the room. Jim's irises contracted to pinholes as his bloodshot eyes reeled to process what they were seeing. He was blinded. A silhouette at first. Then, Lydia walked out.

"Good. You're awake. You're an animal! I'm actually sore. Thanks for the romp. We should do breakfast tomorrow. My treat!", she said as she scurried out of the room wrapped in a towel.

Jim hadn't even processed all that had happened before the door to his room clicked shut. Jim sat up on the edge of the bed. He looked at the night stand at the other line of cocaine he'd laid out. It sat there still, perfectly straight and untouched.

19.

Heads

The house was an ordinary one. It sat in the middle of the block, in the middle of the development, in the middle of suburbia. There was nothing remarkable about the house. It looked like all its neighbors and you would never have stopped to give it a second thought. Tonight, this ordinary house stood silent, dark. Only one light could be seen from the street, in the front window.

Edgar and his wife sat inside their ordinary house. The house itself was quiet too. No TV played. No music played and Edgar and his wife were too expectant to talk to each other. The wait had been long. They hadn't slept much in the last eighteen hours. They were older, not accustomed to this shift in their routine and the effect was noticeable on both of them. Their eyes were tired and their motions slower than normal. They sat next to each other, on the silk sofa, in the tastefully decorated home in the middle of the block, in the middle of the development in the middle of suburbia under a silent moonless night in their dark quiet house. The air was still as they waited.

The ringing of the phone punctured the silence like the roar of a cannon. To the tired, expectant ears of Edgar and his wife, the ringing was deafening and the pulses from the ringer of the phone hit them like the ripples of a sonic boom.

They looked at each other. They looked at the phone. Neither one of them moved. There in that house, they were safe. No news is good news and as long as neither of them picked up the phone, their world was intact, life was normal and they could go on.

But the phone kept ringing.

Paralyzed by fear in those moments between one ring of the bell on the phone and the next, they sat not moving.

It must have overwhelmed Edgar and inside his heart he found the courage to stand up and look fate in the eye. He rose. His legs seemed like lead as he dragged them over the plush, cream colored carpet towards the incessantly ringing black phone with its piercing metallic bell. He had to know. Fate he could deal with, but the unknowing, the swinging of his mind between extremes that fate could take and the sleepless nights were too much for him. Best to get it over with and know, rather than suffer more of the sleepless nights, lying motionless next to his crying wife.

A wound would heal and life would go on, but the not knowing tore the wound open every moment of the tortured day. He had to know.

Edgar had dragged his motionless feet across the width of the room and stood next to the incessantly ringing phone. His nerve was ebbing, but he had enough left to carry him over the top. He reached out with a trembling hand and lifted the receiver to his ear.

The voice on the other end of the line spoke. Edgar listened.

He hung up the phone. He hung his head low. He couldn't bear to look his wife in her pleading eyes yet. His courage was a;; but gone, but there was enough for this final act before he collapsed, fearful and timid again. Time for one more bit of stoicism, for her.

"The found Josh. He was in the river. That was the morgue. They need us to come and identify the body."

Tears rolled down Edgar's face as he fell into his wife's mournful, supportive embrace.

20.

Tails

The house was an ordinary one. It sat in the middle of the block, in the middle of the development, in the middle of suburbia. There was nothing remarkable about the house. It looked like all its neighbors and you would never have stopped to give it a second thought. Tonight, this ordinary house stood silent, dark. Only one light could be seen from the street, in the front window.

Edgar and his wife sat inside their ordinary house. The house itself was quiet too. No TV played. No music played and Edgar and his wife were too expectant to talk to each other. The wait had been long. They hadn't slept much in the last eighteen hours. They were older, not accustomed to this shift in their routine and the effect was noticeable on both of them. Their eyes were tired and their motions slower than normal. They sat next to each other, on the silk sofa, in the tastefully decorated home in the middle of the block, in the middle of the development in the middle of suburbia under a silent moonless night in their dark quiet house. The air was still as they waited.

The ringing of the phone punctured the silence like the roar of a cannon. To the tired, expectant ears of Edgar and his wife, the ringing was deafening and the pulses from the ringer of the phone hit them like the ripples of a sonic boom.

They looked at each other. They looked at the phone. Neither one of them moved. There in that house, they were safe. No news is good news and as long as neither of them picked up the phone, their world was intact, life was normal and they could go on.

But the phone kept ringing.

Paralyzed by fear in those moments between one ring of the bell on the phone and the next, they sat not moving.

It must have overwhelmed Edgar and inside his heart he found the courage to stand up and look fate in the eye. He rose. His legs seemed like lead as he dragged them over the plush, cream colored carpet towards the incessantly ringing black phone with its piercing metallic bell. He had to know. Fate he could deal with, but the unknowing, the swinging of his mind between extremes that fate could take and the sleepless nights were too much for him. Best to get it over with and know, rather than suffer more of the sleepless nights, lying motionless next to his crying wife.

A wound would heal and life would go on, but the not knowing tore the wound open every moment of the tortured day. He had to know.

Edgar had dragged his motionless feet across the width of the room and stood next to the incessantly ringing phone. His nerve was all but gone, but he had enough left to carry him over the top. He reached out with a trembling hand and lifted the receiver to his ear.

The voice on the other end of the line spoke. Edgar listened.

He hung up the phone. He looked at his wife. He looked at her in her pleading, desperate eyes as tears began to well up in his own. His courage was gone, it had been used up in lifting the phone. Now all that remained was the vacuum in his soul that was left as the fear evaporated. It was going to be OK.

"That was the doctor. The results are in and it's negative."

Tears rolled down both their joyous faces as they fell into a supportive, comforting, grateful embrace.

21.

Guillame

Guillame awoke on a hard, dirt floor with a pounding head. It throbbed. He had drank too much in the tavern the night before and his body reeled from the overexertion. This was no way to live. It wasn't even the first time he had woken up on a floor that week. That didn't alarm him as much as one might have suspected.

He sat up and looked around. Somehow, it was different. Where was he? What had happened? His foggy head tried to make sense of the room he was in and tried to surmise just how he might have come to be there.

It was not a large room. He suspected that it might be ten feet by ten feet square. All the walls were constructed of dark, worn red brick with the look of having been in place for a century. It was no room Guillame had ever seen before and he grew more curious. His eyes moved from corner to corner in the room looking for a door, an entrance, a window. There was nothing. The walls all displayed a common uniformity and none showed a manner of egress.

His eyes began to adjust and to Guillame's horror, he

realized his body, garments, hair and even his face were covered in insects. They were crawling over him, small clawed legs tickling every patch of skin they touched. They made his skin crawl. He shot up with a fervor of muscle contractions and sprang to his feet and began frantically swiping his hands over his whole self to remove the filthy little creatures.

What was this place?

He looked around with greater drive now as a sense of being trapped began to creep into his mind. As far as he could tell, he was in no immediate danger, but claustrophobia had always been one of Guillame's weaknesses. He could feel his skin, now free of the vermin, begin to grow cold, clammy and moist as fear began to seep into his consciousness. Panic would not be far behind. He needed to master himself now so he could find the exit he had used as an entrance soon.

A small oil lamp hung from what appeared to be a rusted iron hook in the the ceiling and lit the room with soft, flickering light. The ceiling appeared to be made of slabs of stone of some sort. He knocked on them. They were solid. The walls too were solid. He stamped the dirt floor with his feet. It was thickly packed, solid like clay and had been undisturbed for eons.

He began to trace the perimeter of the room, running his hands over the worn, eroded bricks looking for the way he had come into this room. One wall. Another. The third. He stopped. One brick protruded from the wall. It was half out like someone had slipped it back into the wall after pulling it out. On the brick, written in white chalk was the word "Guillame".

Guillame fell to his feet. He clawed at the brick with no care to the pain it brought to his finger nails. Panic was with him now. Desperation and madness would follow. Time was short. This was something, something that might offer him liberty. He pulled it out. There was nothing behind it but a small recess and a worn piece of folded paper. He took it out and opened it.

"Welcome to your crypt Guillame. There is no exit. Go with God. The carrion beetles I left with you will have stripped your bones clean by the time I return. You will make a lovely skeleton in a classroom somewhere. I promise you that."

The letter was signed "A friend you made into an enemy"

22.

The Raid

The bolts of the twin Lewis gun in front of him were cocked back, locked, ready to fire. Sergeant Stafford, breathed slowly, patiently. This wasn't the first time. He knew what to do and he knew what to expect. Corporal Mulligan sat behind him, likewise, nonchalantly with his hands on the grip of his own machine gun. He too, was ready. The engine purred, almost mutely. Lieutenant White's foot was on the clutch, his hand on the gear shifter ready to send the jeep hurtling forward. All they needed were the flares. The flares would start the show.

They'd been in the desert for weeks, acting as honorary Bedouin. Their beards were long and full, their uniforms dusty, their skin the leathery brown that Englishmen turn when they live under an unforgiving African sun. They had even adopted the kafiyahs worn by the Bedouins themselves. They looked more like pirates afloat in a sea of sand than they did soldiers of His Majesty's armed forces in Egypt. Yet, they were.

They, were, in fact, vital to the war effort. Since the Afrika Korps had crossed the Mediterranean, it had been one reverse after another. The whole of the British front had been pushed back along the winding highways that bordered the sea. Now, the Germans threatened the fatal drive into Egypt, and the severance of the Canal which would condemn Great Britain to the slow death a lack of oil would bring. To slow down and harass this effort, was what these men, and the rest of their small unit had been sent behind German lines to do.

It was a new kind of war, and it required new tactics. They had gone native, assumed the habits of those who called the desert home and had gone to work, bringing grief to the Germans in anyway they could. Now, they waited in the dark for the flares that would start the latest action, an attack on a forward air base that had been menacing British positions up and down the line. They'd found the hated Stukas in their nest three days ago. They'd stalked them like animals and now they waited for the kill. All they needed were the flares.

The strontium flares shattered the darkness of the noir night with the intensity of the noon day sun. Lieutenant White needed no coaxing. His muscles had been twitching, waiting, like a runner for the crack of the gun. He knew what to do without thinking about it. It was muscle memory by now. The jeep sprinted forward at the behest of his automatic movements, across the desert toward the wire of the base. Other men from their team, sappers, had cut the wire, just before the flares and the path was open now.

Dust trailed the jeep as it hurtled towards the planes, helplessly lining the runway. The Germans hadn't even bothered to fortify them. Hubris. They sat, exposed to the murderous fire of Mulligan and Stafford. Chaos ran rampant inside the wire. Men were running to and fro, amid the confusion as a red, orange, swirling, towering fireball shot into the sky. The other team had hit the fuel dump, as planned. Men were running to put out the fire. No one paid attention to the jeep speeding through the compound. They moved almost invisibly as fast as the engine's pistons could propel them.

Mulligan and Stafford held their fire. They were experienced men. They knew their weapons could only fire a few seconds worth of deadly shot and they wanted the planes, specifically the engines. Their discipline maintained as the jeep whizzed down the runway. Bullets were headed their way now. The defenders knew what was happening and some of them had managed to begin to mount a defense. It was too late. They were in, and their prey was at the mercy of a now withering fire. Stafford took the left, Mulligan the right.

The noise was deafening. Four barrels, firing 600 rounds per minutes. The concussion unbearable. Stafford could feel his teeth rattling as bursts of flame shot, continuously from his weapon. The whole chaotic scene grew mute between the bursts and the brilliant flashes. He heard nothing. Hot shells from Mulligans weapon landed on him, burned him. He kept spurting bullets, following the red dashes of tracer fire into the engines of the hated planes. Their war was over now. One of the engines exploded in a burst of flame. The acrid smoke of the fuel it contained billowed out in thick plumes of black as the jeep headed for the other end of the runway, toward the wire again. The burning hulks of once terrible monsters left dead in their wake. They'd done what they could, they'd hurt the Boshe. Their work done, it was a soldier's duty to get out and live to fight another day.

They hurtled back out through the hole in the wire, an expanding trail of dust following them. A few parting shots as they drove off into the moonless night. No ill effect. The defenders hadn't had enough time to hurt them. They'd been in the compound less than a minute, yet the fires would burn hot all night.

23.

Another Raid

I was so nervous. My palms were sweaty. I couldn't go back empty handed. I'd talked it up. I'd bragged. They were waiting outside. I'd said I could deliver and now I'd gone too far to stop.

I opened the sticky, red door. The smell was instant. Cigarette smoke and sweat. A potpourri made over years. I hooked to the left, trying to be discreet. I hoped the tattooed, long haired man behind the counter would be too apathetic to give me a second glance. He was. He swung a mop on a daily basis.

I cut through the arcade. It was a tunnel. A dark tunnel with numbered doors to private booths. I always wondered, curiously, what kind of sinful, forbidden deeds happened behind those black numbered doors with brass handles. I never looked at the floor but my shoes always stuck to it. No time to stop and wonder today. I was on a mission.

I made it to the racks. Around the corner were the girls waiting for someone to dance for. If only I had the money. I didn't. A movie was going to have to do. We'd all chipped in. It was a community effort.

My heart was pumping in my chest even though the tattooed man couldn't see me now. I could shop, but not for long. They were waiting and my pride was on the line and lunch period only lasted so long. I scanned the oversized, greasy, empty VHS boxes. I looked. I studied the tantalizing preview pictures of the movies. I made my selection.

Go time. Put up or shut up. I took a deep breath and I walked around the counter to pay. A another deep breath. The panic. There were two long haired, tattooed men at the counter now and only one underage Catholic high schooler in the shop. No turning back. They were still waiting.

"Fortune favors the bold." I thought to myself.

I walked up to the counter. I played it cool. I slid the empty box of my selection onto the fingerprint smudged counter that held the really exotic lubes, toys and creams. I looked him in the eyes, willing him to be cool and not ask any questions. Looking away would imply fear, so I stared.

"ID?", he said.

"I left it at home."

It was a tired, tried and empty response. He had to know I

was lying. He looked at the other, until then, silent tattooed man. He was fatter than the other. His t-shirt was more stained and worn.

"It's cool. He's been here before.", He said with a shrug of his shoulders.

Apparently, they knew me. It was cool.

I paid with the crumpled twenty dollar bill. He grabbed the numbered cassette from behind the counter and slid it into the sticky box. There seemed to be a film on everything in the red light bulb lit store. He slid me the nondescript black plastic bag. It hid my prize from the world. He slid me the change. I wondered what those tired one dollar bills he handed me had seen. I smiled at the imagined depravity, a virgin's imagination spinning wild.

It felt like I ran, but I walked calmly outside. They wouldn't bother stopping me now. I was on my way out. The light of the crisp, cold, sunny day hurt my eyes after having been in the store.

My friends came from around the corner. I beamed. I handed one of them the bag. He opened it. They peered in. Then looked at me – disappointed. I thought we were all into chicks with dicks. I was, but I was wrong about them.

In hindsight, we should've talked about it before.

We'd cut school, but the lessons hadn't stopped.

24.

The Box

She'd been in that box for what seemed like forever. She'd been minding her business when a pair of strong hands had grabbed her and thrust her in there. There'd been a tumult. She'd tried to fight. She'd tried to get away, to run, but she was caught by those hands. It was over in seconds. Her world went black as she was roughly handled and knocked about.

She'd awoken in that box. It was dark and cold. So cold, she was sleepy. Her hairs stood on end in that frigid cold. She was used to sun and warmth. She was scared. She didn't know what had happened. She didn't know where she was. The constant rocking made her ill.

She groped around inside her box. It was big enough to walk around in and she felt every edge, every corner and seam looking for a way out. There was nothing. She was trapped. Alone in the dark and cold. Just a gentle rocking, back and forth like the swaying of a hammock.

She lost track of time. With no sun to set apart the days, she had no idea how long she'd been there. She just lay in the corner, huddled, trying to stay warm. Her hairs bristled and she pulled her limbs together to conserve heat. No food came. Nothing but silence and cold. She waited, hoping for a chance of escape. She was confined, trapped in the dark but she never lost hope. She was strong and proud. She would wait for her chance, and if it came, she would be ready.

Evan walked up to the crate and began to open it. He was doing his job, like every other day. He hated it. He wanted to be a writer. This was not how he had envisioned his life working out. He took out his knife.

He cut the seal and opened the container. She was inside, waiting, accustomed to the dark and aware that the box was opening.

As the box opened, light flooded in. It hurt her eyes. She hadn't seen light in many days, but that wasn't going to stop her. She was ready. He muscles tightened, contracted and she rushed toward the light. This was her chance, maybe her only one, and she wasn't going to miss it.

As she burst into the light, her eyes met Evan's.

Evan started and fell back against the worn white walls of the room. Terrified. What was that? He'd always been terrified of spiders and that was the biggest he'd ever seen. He was breathing heavily. What the fuck? It had to be four inches across. Where the fuck had it gone?

"They can wait on bananas." Evan said, hyperventilating. "I need a cigarette. Fuck this job."

He walked outside. As he did, her eight eyes followed him from the shadowy corner of the room with the worn white walls. She'd waited and been ready. She was exhausted. She ached, but she was free.

She wasn't sure what part he'd played in her abduction, but she'd deal with him when he returned.

25.

The Chase

There it was again. That car. By now, Tom was certain it was him. He was always there, two cars behind and it had been over twenty miles. For some reason tonight, of all nights, Tom's eyes had darted to the mirror and watched that reflection, even though the reflected headlights hurt his eyes. He'd been right to do so. There he was again. Tom was sure it was him. He was as persistent as a bloodhound trying to run him to ground, and all over two thousand bucks.

He wanted his money. Tom had borrowed it for a business – of sorts. Not strictly legal. He had always been good at convincing people to invest in his get rich quick schemes. People naturally just wanted to believe, believe fortune would smile on them for taking the risk. It was easy if you knew that. Tom had meant to pay him back, he'd meant to make things work and he'd planned on it. It was just that things went wrong. One thing after another fell out of place. Amateurs meddling in a business of professionals frequently go broke and drugs is a business of professionals. Now that isn't to say the man in the other car was a professional. He was just as much an amateur as Tom, that's why he trusted him in the first place and why he wasn't going to get his money tonight.

Tom wasn't sure what he was planning. He just didn't like the look of it. It could be threats. It could be pleading. It could be awkward or it could be violent. The voice mails had gotten progressively worse and hinted at desperation. One way or the other, this wasn't going to work out and Tom needed to lose this guy and lose him soon before he found out where Tom lived.

Tom's eyes had done their job and seen this man, but now that he knew he was there, Tom didn't know what to do. He'd seen movies. He was no stranger to a car chase, but he had no idea how to get rid of one. He couldn't get him to flip his car over like on TV.

Tom fumbled in his jacket pocket and found his phone. He dialed. 911.

"911. What's your emergency?" The charming female voice on the other end asked.

"I'm being followed on the bridge. I think it's my wife's ex-husband. He's threatened to hurt me. He has a gun and I don't know what to do. I need help."

It was all a lie. Tom wasn't married. His fake wife had no ex-husband and the non-existent ex-husband had no gun. That was OK. The phone was a disposable and Tom felt good about the lie. He sold it.

"Please help me." he followed up, a tinge of faux panic in his voice.

Tom should have been an actor.

Tom followed her instructions. He kept talking to her, hamming it up, sounding like a panic attack would soon

overwhelm him. He got off the freeway and kept talking.
He turned and twisted as the operator guided in his relief.
Police can be very helpful in a pinch if you have a
disposable cell phone.

The other man was still there, he'd followed every twist and
turn, still a few car lengths back. So close.

Tom smiled and silently cackled to himself when the police
car behind the other man lit up and silhouetted the rage of
his pursuer in red and blue light. It was over. He'd lost.
Tom had won.

"Thank you officer. Thank you for your help." Tom
stammered out, over mock tears as he hung up the phone
and laughed self indulgently at his own selfish cleverness.

26.

The Big Day

Nathan nervously pressed his foot on the accelerator and
the beaten up old minivan exited the parking lot onto the
busy avenue. He was nervous. He'd waited a long time for
this and he was filled with angst.

He reached for the turn signal and signed to the other
motorists that he was moving to the right. The lane change

was perfectly executed. The van was moving now, faster as it moved to catch up to the other motorists. Smooth sailing now. Now, he just needed to stay calm, get it over with and it would be a good day. He breathed a sigh of relief.

Things were going great. He was catching all greens and the van was moving along at a good clip. Through the crosswalk and past the high school it went. He was in a hurry now. He wanted to get this done and get on with the day.

The light in the intersection turned yellow just as the red minivan sailed underneath it. It had been green when he entered the intersection and hadn't noticed. It was OK, but his luck was changing and he didn't even know it. Forces were conspiring against him and he had already lost, but he kept trying, oblivious to that fact.

Shortly ahead of the van, he could see the next intersection. The light was green. He could see the crosswalk signs beginning to flash their orange warnings. The light would change soon. He needed to make it. He had to make it through that intersection. Without even realizing it, his foot became heavier, pressed down on the accelerator and urged the van forward. His speed was up there now. Five over the limit. He didn't notice. Ten over. He wouldn't have cared anyway. He had to make that light. It wasn't necessary, but he wanted it.

The light turned yellow and he didn't stop. He had to make it. He flew through the intersection just as the light turned red. It was good! He'd made it. He was sure of that.

"Pull over now!" the until then, silent, West African in the passenger seat commanded in a voice tinged with an irritated French accent.

Nathan snapped back to reality. He'd been in his head. He'd forgotten the West African.

"Sir. You have just completed a moving violation. By regulation, this driver's exam is now concluded and you have failed."

Nathan, sitting in the parked car in the taco restaurant parking lot took out the keys. He handed them towards the West African man with the French accent in disgrace. The man just shook his head side to side disapprovingly.

"No." he said "You still drive us back. A licensed driver will need to drive you home."

Nathan understood. This one was not going to go over well. He could lie to his mother. He could tell her something that would placate her. He could try again for the test in 30 days. His girlfriend was a different matter. She wouldn't care why he had failed. She would just know that he had failed and that she was going to have to pick him up for another 30 days. No way he was getting that promised blowjob. That was out. He sighed and started the car.

27.

An Innocent Incident

I'd asked Kate out a few days before. She lived in the dorms and I'd been in there studying economics with my friend Tommy. I knew her. I'd seen her around. She knew me. She was everything a college sophomore wants. She was hot. She wanted to be a nurse or something. Honestly, I didn't pay attention. I wasn't looking for a life partner. I just wanted to get laid like any other red blooded American man in college.

I'd popped my head in her open dorm. Real casual. Like you would imagine some suave, sexy movie star doing. I made a little small talk and then, ever so casually, like I didn't care what her answer was. I asked her if she wanted to double with Tommy and I on Saturday. I did it just like I'd practiced. A double date is usually best. It makes her more comfortable. No one ever gets raped on a double date. She said yes and my head filled with visions of motorboating those great big boobs of hers.

Saturday night rolled around. I spent a little time primping. I'd never admit to that if you knew my name, but I did and you don't. Guys like to look good too. What if I met a better girl than Katie while we were out? I needed to look good to be smooth. Tommy came by my off campus apartment. Katie and her friend (Tommy's date) were going to swing by and pick us up.

Katie called me up on my cell. They were outside. I let them wait a minute. Women don't want a man who looks too eager. Tommy and I took a minute. Then we headed downstairs. We got outside. It was early in the school year. The leaves were turning and the night was crisp under a dark, cloudy sky. It was a perfect night for motorboating and red blooded American college first date sex. The college experience, dorm life and college girls are wonderful things.

I had to fart. Better to do it before I was in the car to stink up the night air with the remnants of lunch. Enchilada farts in a hatchback could be a big deal breaker. I squeezed. I farted.

I shit.

I froze. All I could do was think "OH FUCK I JUST SHIT MY PANTS". Twenty one years of life, high school sports, the scouts, my parents, church, all of it had failed to prepare me for this moment. I had nothing. The playbook in my head was blank. Me, standing there with Tommy in the car with Katie and her girlfriend and me, with wet, shit filled boxer briefs that I was pretty sure had already seeped through my pants. I couldn't sit. I knew my face was telegraphing everything that was happening in my pants and in my head as poo ran down my legs. I had to do something. I did something. I panicked.

I ran. I just ran. I didn't say anything. I didn't make an excuses. I just turned around and ran into the night. Motorboating was out. Katie was out. Getting laid was out – for tonight. If the story got around about what happened, I would have to transfer. I'd have to start over. Go to a remote school somewhere in Albania where no one could find me. I'd be that guy who shit his pants. That guy gets no pussy - ever.

I ran. I just ran. My legs made the decision before my mind had a chance to agree. Billions of years of survival programming took over and muscles that wanted a chance to get laid again, rather than be ruined contracted, flexed and moved me on their own. I don't remember where I ran. All I remember of the actual running was the cool autumn air filling my lungs and the drizzly rain spattering in my face, forming droplets on my nose. I ran with every ounce of unconscious, survival mode strength I had inside me. I do know it made the incident in my pants all the messier at that point. But it was too late to care about all of that.

I hopped a fence and landed in a pile of wet, rotting leaves and hid, motionless. From what Tommy later told me, they looked for me for a while and finally gave up.

I got home. I snuck in like I was robbing the place instead of just going home. I cleaned up the disaster in my pants, threw the clothes into a black plastic bag I tied in a very tight knot. Later, I walked the bag, discreetly in my backpack, to the dumpster behind the commons like the dirty secret it was. I threw it in wrapped in a black plastic bag tied in a knot like all dirty secrets in a dumpster.

Tommy was cool once I told him the details about the whole sordid affair. He could know. Tommy and I were like brothers. Katie, that was different. I made up a story. I called Katie three days later. I told her I had taken some mushrooms before the date and they had hit me moments before she pulled up in the car. I told her a lot of swirling, psychedelic details about the only too real horrors I saw in that car when she pulled up. Made the whole little incident into a bad trip. She understood. She laughed at me. I could tell over her giggles that she thought I was a maverick or a wild man and that intrigued her. She even agreed to go out with me again.

College girls are great.

28.

You Can't See My Teeth?

Did you just call me sweetheart? Can't see my teeth? Can't see my fucking teeth? What a fucking cunt. Ha ha. Very funny. You can't see my teeth because I'm not smiling. I get it. I get it now. Thanks for explaining that. Would you be smiling if you had to get up every day, come to a job you hate and wait on stupid uptight cunts like yourself? Probably not.

You think just because you sit at one of my tables and order some overpriced Cobb salad that you get to talk to me like some sort of shit you scraped off your shoe? You think just because I'm at work and my boss is watching and I need this job to make rent with my four fucking roommates that I won't say anything?

Well, you're right. I need this fucking job you whore. I fucking need it and I have to take shit from cunts like you all the time. I can't call home to Ohio again and ask my parents for money. I'm here, I'm living paycheck to paycheck in a job I hate. Liberal arts degrees don't cut it. You have fun at college and then you get a job waiting on cunts. That's it. That's me. That's my fucking life.

You know, I fucking hate you, but there is a little part of me that sympathizes with you. If I was some stuck up cunt always worried about what everyone thought of me, living for appearances I would be a bitch too. I mean, I can only imagine the inexhaustible well of sadness that must live inside your icy core that you need to come and bust some pathetic waitress' balls. I mean really, how fucked up must your life be?

Sure, your husband is probably tired of coming to bed with an oyster shucker to pry that dried up old clam of yours open. You're jealous of me. That's it. I'm cute with a great ass. Yes, he's probably banging that hot secretary that you saw at the Christmas party and you're taking it out on me. Yes, she was flirting with him. I know how much that must eat you up inside. You're aging like milk. You, know that he is just biding his time until the kids are in college and he can work up the courage to leave you for her and go buy a motorcycle. Then what will you do? You'll just be some dried up old bitter troll with an expensive hair do that you think everyone is noticing. By the way, it makes you look like some washed up, old country music singer who we are all feeling sorry for anyway.

What are you anyway? Just some real estate agent? Dressed up faux fancy thinking you are impressing everyone. Look, the truth is that if you're acting as some house pimp to a bunch of old money spoiled brats, they already know what you are. They know you don't make shit, have to put on airs and look like you know how to be fancy and look like you have money. So you've got a sexy Japanese car? Real money drives Italian. But, the truth is, you pay your bills just like everyone else you fake ice queen. I hate you.

I'm being too hard on you. I'm sure you have it tough. I mean, just think about your kids. Those pretentious, spoiled little bastards. Do you even know who the father is on the first one? Are you sure it's the asshole you married or did you just pick him out of the three and he was too stupid to get a test. I mean they're almost grown. They're almost gone. Look, you failed. They suck. You hate 'em. I know. I can see the look of failure in your eyes and you're hoping that I don't notice so you put on some kind of show. You bust my balls in the hopes that I won't notice what you see in the mirror every morning. A worthless, fucked out shell that's no good to anyone and someone who should just go and kill themselves. It'll save everyone a lot of headache.

Look. Again, I'm being too hard on you. Your life sucks. I'm not going to make a scene. I couldn't if I wanted to. I need this job. You've got me there. But I will give you a tip even if you won't give me one. Don't say you're going to stiff me until after I give you your food and drinks. I can't make a scene, but I can do awful things to your coffee.

Hope you like your coffee you dried up, worthless cunt. The soup will be even better. I promise.

29.

Fate's Recompense

It was a terrible prison full of small, terrible cells. It was cold, dank and even the concrete walls were rotting like the men who sat in those cells whiling away their time. The worst of them were locked in the wing that held inmates waiting execution. They were bad men. They had done terrible things and they had hurt many people. They deserved whatever punishment had been assigned to them. They would die horribly at the hands of avenging justice.

That was true of all of them, except one.

There was an innocent man awaiting execution in one of those terrible cells, in the cold, dank, filthy prison with crumbling walls. He had not done what he was accused of. He had never hurt anyone. He had lived a virtuous life and now sat innocent, yet condemned to a horrible death anyway. He waited stoically for his end. It would come, it was only a matter of time.

He had protested his innocence. He had cooperated fully with the forces of Justice believing that Fate would never turn her back on an innocent, virtuous man. His cooperation had only made it easier for the forces of Justice to prove his guilt. They were wrong, he was innocent, but he was condemned anyway, to the festering prison to rot while they prepared the elaborate means to bring about his end.

He had not been wrong, however. Fate does not turn her back from the virtuous and the innocent. Yes, he had been found guilty, and yes he had been condemned to a horrible, most likely slow death, but she had not turned from him.

Sometimes, in rare circumstances where the virtuous have fallen afoul of Justice, Fate will intervene directly.

Fate is a special thing. She is the unseen force that normally guides the destinies of men, women, nations and peoples. She raises those deserving of merit, the righteous and the deserving and throws down the wicked, the villainous and the cruel. Normally, Fate is unseen, unperceived and unnoticed. But, now and again, in special instances, Fate can become manifest, present herself to those who have been wronged and offer special consideration to undo wrongs.

This was one of those times. An innocent man, condemned to a horrible, slow death for a sin uncommitted was more than Fate could tolerate. Fate elected to appear to this innocent man, and offer him respite from all the wrongs he suffered.

In that cell, in that rotting prison one night, Fate did indeed become manifest to the innocent, wronged and forgotten man. She appeared like she often does, as an amorphous force, truly one of the clockwork gears of creation, spinning us all around in a machinery beyond our comprehension. She was present, felt, yet beyond the understanding of the simple, innocent man.

"You have been wronged. You have been virtuous. I am here to correct that."

The words rang out in a powerful, haunting, unheard voice in the man's mind.

"I will grant one wish. Any wish you desire as recompense for your lifetime of good. Choose!" again, words unheard thundered in his mind.

He didn't need to think long. He knew what to do. He spoke.

"I want to be the judge in a blowjob contest between two beautiful women. I'm thinking redheads." He roared out to the unseen ears of Fate.

Anyone outside his cell would have thought him mad, to hear him carrying on.

Fate was stunned. She had assumed a man like this would wish for freedom, justice and liberty.

"Are you sure?" a rarely hesitant Fate asked in softer, uncertain, unspoken words in the condemned man's mind.

"Of course. One way or another, I am going to die. It's certain. However, to be the judge in a blowjob contest, that is a dream that many man would seek and few would achieve. Were this to be granted, I would happily go to the scaffold a hundred times as an innocent man. My life would end, but what a life it would have been!"

Fate granted the wish without further discussion, and the next day, the man died a horrible, slow death with an unexplained, misunderstood smile permanently fixed across his lips.

30.

A Counseling Session

Edith was a divorcee and a devoted parishioner. Every week, she was one of the first people in St. Matthew's. She sat in the front pew, listened intently and gave what she could to the parish. Father Michaels, was a young priest, younger than Edith by at least ten years. He had excelled at seminary, studied in Rome and was a rising star in the diocese.

Edith had come to Father Michaels' office to talk. Since her divorce, she had had trouble making sense of her place in the world. Her faith had been tested, not destroyed, and Father Michaels had been a lighthouse on her stormy seas. He had helped her to find her way, to make peace with herself and her cheating husband and to accept where her life stood. They had met weekly. Both had come to look forward to their time together. Edith would even go as far as to bring Father Micahels batches of her "famous" cookies that were all the rave at church fundraisers. He did have a sweet tooth after all.

The day had started like any other. She had brought cookies, he'd made tea and small talk had ensued. He had been reaching for a book on the shelf in his rectory, to give her something to study over the next week. That's when he had turned around and found her there, face to face with him. He could feel her breath. She was breathing hard from excitement, anticipation and the fear that her nerves might fail her or what she planned might come to not.

She kissed him. She kissed him with the gratitude that all these many months of his help had built up inside her. It was understandable. However, at the same time, her kiss contained all the lust that had frothed in her mind about Father Michaels. He was young, attractive, and loving, yet commanding, dominant and supple. She hadn't made love since Dan had left her. She'd been untouched. She wanted this man, forbidden or not, to touch her, badly. He saw it in her eyes and he needed little persuading. He was a priest, not a dead man.

He grabbed her shoulders in his large hands and pulled her to him. She submitted as her own hands reached out and touched his hips, urging him closer. She pulled his hips to her own. He began to push her back and moved with her, all the time kissing her. Edith bumped into his desk, and moving on instinct, sat down on it. She began to undo his buttons and exposed his chest. She paused at the collar, but her weakened faith was not enough to stop her. The priest, was not inexperienced and knew what to do. His long suppressed lust needed little encouragement. He hiked up Edith's dress to find nothing stood between him and the temptation that lay between her thighs only garters to hold up her stockings. She pulled open his black trousers and they gave in to temptation together.

For Edith, the feeling of someone inside her after all these months was electric. Life was being breathed back into her. His touch was warm, loving and gentle, yet at the same time masculine and commanding. She could feel the muscles of his back, tight, as he braced himself on the desk. Her nails dug in. For now, he was hers. He slid in and out with ease as she lurched her hips to meet each thrust. Finally he cried out and fell limply onto her. He lay there, inside her, as they breathed deeply - together.

It was over quickly. Sin is a powerful aphrodisiac. But at

least this week, Edith would have something to talk about, while giggling, with her favorite confessor.

31.

A Helo Conversation

Three of them went up in the bird with us. They'd been caught in the wire the night before. They'd tripped a flare. There had been five. Now there were three. Two of them laid out there rotting where the gunners had put them down the night before. No burial detail had been assigned. No time. These men had been mapping the perimeter, looking for the automatics, looking for weakness. Something was coming. They were coming and if they'd been that bold, they were coming soon. We needed to know what they knew and we needed to know it fast. Lives were at stake – ours.

The blades of the helo roared as the engine throttle opened and tons of steel climbed into the ever hot, ever humid air. We climbed. The landscape below grew amorphous, peaceful and even beautiful. From the air it was always peaceful. I was witnessing. Someone higher than me was conducting the interrogation. He knew what to ask. This was his show. I wasn't even supposed to be there.

108

We were high before I knew it. The doors opened and the downdraft of the rotors filled the cabin. Below, green fields and dusty brown mingled as far as you could see. A mottled patchwork of wild and cultivated lands. Rolling hills under a darkening gray sky.

They were facing into the cabin. They didn't need to look outside. They knew where they were. They knew what was going to happen. They were poor. They were uneducated. They weren't stupid. They knew what to expect. They'd lived with the threats and consequences of violence their whole lives.

My superior began talking. He was bombastic and moved his hands a lot. He was intimidating. He put on a show trying to make these three men feel small. He wanted them afraid. That was how we got what we needed. Then it happened. The man closest to the tail, on his knees got a push. He screamed as he went out the door. Everyone screams when they go out the door of an aircraft without a chute, even the most defiant. It's just natural. From my jump seat, I watched him fall as far as I could before I lost sight of him. We didn't need to know where he landed. No one was going to pick him up, but at a point, you watch. Its not horrible. Its just curious. A curious spectacle of a man silently, seemingly slowly floating his way down to Earth.

The other two were breathing harder now. This wasn't a game. The third man hadn't been asked questions. He'd gone out to show that we weren't fucking around. It wasn't just another scare tactic. It was a lethal part of the show. We wanted them to know, then and there that if they held back, there would be real consequences.

The questions started flowing. Staccato, angry words. They flowed fast, filling the cabin. They were arguing back and forth. Tell me! No! The second man went out the door and again, I watched his silhouette as he flailed, helplessly kicking his legs, as far as I could. He just blended in and he was gone. I chewed my gum and kept watching from behind my sunglasses. This went on for some time. I'd grown cold to this sort of thing by then. Emotions were off. It was business. Ask questions and send them out when you're done. They were never coming back down, alive anyway.

More questions. More sharp, angry responses and frustration. It wasn't getting us anywhere. They were tough. They were hard men. They were used to this. They were used to brutality. Even now, in the helicopter, the third man's eyes were filled with a steely defiance. He hated us. He would've killed us without thought if he could have. But he couldn't. He was bound and powerless now.

My superior punched him. Shouted at him. The man's face was a bloody, pulpy mess after a time. Nothing. He looked up. We were all calm. This was routine. He spat in the face of his interrogator. Rage washed over the inquisitor's face and he kicked the third, obstinate man out of the open door. He was finished with him. He too fell. Three men. Three men dead and we hadn't gotten anything. We knew their friends were coming. We'd prepare anyway. We hadn't expected much. They rarely talked.

We usually got their deaths long before we got their obedience.

32.

The White Door

I stood staring at that white door for what seemed to be forever. Fortuitously, or maybe not so much, the number on the door was thirteen.

"Why not?" I thought to myself.

It seemed perfect. The number on the door was bad luck. She should've realized it when she moved in. Not my fault she was under a bad star. It didn't change anything. I was there to upset her. There was no getting around that. It wasn't her fault. It was his. She was as much a victim as I was. Whatever she thought when she got out of bed that morning, she was going to have a whole new, bad worldview when her head hit the pillow that night. It couldn't be helped. It was going to be unpleasant, but she deserved to know and I was going to tell her.

I rang the door bell. Immediately, inside the apartment, I could hear the yapping of a small, annoying dog. Why is it every other woman I know has a small annoying dog these days? It's an accessory, just like a purse. I really believe in most cases, they don't even like them. They just feel that they must have one. Somewhere in that apartment, barking its small, furry head off was a small annoying accessory.

"Maybe she's not home." I thought to myself.

What was I supposed to do then? I had worked all of it out, how it was going to work, in my head. I was going to ring the bell, she was going to open it. I was going to say what I'd come to say before I lost my nerve, before I started to cry. But I'd never thought about what I would do if she wasn't home.

Waiting in the car seemed creepy. The doorstep was OK. I had come to say my piece. In the car, in the rain, waiting and watching apartment number thirteen, I was a stalker. I couldn't do that. Somewhere in my mind, there was a distinction. That was going too far. That was crossing a line and I wouldn't feel good about myself. I couldn't do that.

Just as I'd resolved not to stalk and was breaths away from giving up the latch of the door turned with a click. It began to open. The door made the same sucking sound as it opened that all apartment doors seem to make. A pretty brunette stood in the doorway.

She was pretty, but comfortable. Her hair was up. She was in sweats and she wasn't wearing any make up. I'd caught her at rest, at play even. Relaxing, maybe enjoying her day off. I'm sure some guilty pleasure was muted on the TV inside and some fatty snack she would never eat in front of him was next to her fading impression on the couch. Another guilty secret she'd never admit to the world.

We both stood there for a moment, her at rest, me dripping from the hard rain coming down, staring at one another. We seemed to each be considering the other. Eyes blinking. Wheels turned in each of our minds and thoughts raced. Each of us trying to figure out what was going on. Her out of ignorance. Me out of fear.

"Can I help you?" She said, breaking the silence.

I was terrified and shaking. A push of determination from somewhere inside crashed over the breaker.

"Your boyfriend slept with me last month. I thought you should know. It's been eating me up. He told me he was single. I'm so sorry."

The words fell home. Tears welled in her eyes and I turned around and ran back into the wet night. I'd said what needed to be said and then, there, afterwards, I just wanted to run away.

33.

The Weathered Dock

As the boat approached the long, weathered dock, all that could be heard was the sound of the rain. It was coming down in sheets and the sound on the steel roofs of the islands made a deafening white noise. They had come a long way to seek the man in the house and they were soaked. They both wanted it over quickly so they could get home and be done with it. They were like any two men on a business trip.

One of them, Hector, squatted on the bow of the open boat

as it approached the dock. He grabbed one of the worn planks and pulled the boat close. He tied it securely. The other man, Wladimir, did the same with the stern. The two men did this patiently and methodically. They weren't nervous, or in a rush. They'd done this before. They knew their business and they did it well. Jitters and nerves had fallen by the wayside a long time ago.

They had waited to come to this lonely, large hacienda on the bay until the rain had come to this island. Four days spent, impatiently, in a traveler's hostel, telling people they were Venezuelan tourists who lived in San Salvador. No one had asked questions.

Once the boat was secured and wouldn't drift away, Hector handed Wladimir the damp, black canvas bag that contained their tools. Plumbers have wrenches, these two had two antiquated Sten guns. They were old, but reliable and effective. Wladimir opened the bag and slid the magazines into the wells of their weapons and cocked back the bolts. They stood up and started the walk, through the manicured gardens, towards the quiet, sleeping house.

The man sleeping inside with his family was from the States. He didn't know anything about Hector and Wladimir. He didn't know they were there to see him. He was just there to sleep. He'd been busy on a business trip of his own to Costa Rica the last two days, like he did, running packages in his fishing boat. He was really just a well paid courier, an employee like so many others, and he was exhausted. He slept like a dead man.

A landscaper from Houston before, he had come to this island on vacation and had never left. He became a fisherman and for a long time, making his money taking tourists out to where the big tuna swam, and for a while he had been happy. The income was OK, but not great. Enough to live on, but not enough to live the life he wanted. One day, a friend in a bar had offered him work taking periodic trips up the coast with packages. He'd promised money. He'd delivered. The work was easy. Life was better then.

But there had been a problem. One of the last loads was light. There'd been a supply chain problem somewhere. It could have happened anywhere along the line. Off the books "leakage" that happens when precious cargo moves around the world in the hands of smugglers, thieves and criminals. It wasn't the fisherman's fault, but the blame was his none the less. Management wanted a change and two men were walking to the house to inform him of the decision.

116

The brass finished doorknob on the heavy mahogany door of his bedroom silently turned under the din of the rain on the steel roof. It silently opened.

You could see the muzzle flashes that ended the fisherman's life through his bedroom window across the bay. No one saw anything. No one was looking. No one cared. He'd be replaced soon enough. Greedy gringos were never in short supply.

34.

The Flautist

She was a European flautist by training. Somewhere from behind the Iron Curtain. Czech. Maybe, Hungarian. Eurochic no matter how you looked at her. She spoke with an accent, dressed elegantly and smelled of seductive, exotic perfumes.

He had come, like so many before him, because others wanted him to. They wanted him to learn skills that would make him interesting and cultured. He had wanted other options. He'd been offered none. This was what he was to do whether he liked it or not. He acted out. He did not practice. He did not study and it showed. He was impetuous, even defiant.

His apathy had not gone unnoticed. His fingering was sloppy and his ability to read music had hardly developed at all. She could be a savage task mistress at times, but she knew that a pupil was nothing more than another instrument. She was to play him and he was to play his own instrument. Through her to him, to his instrument, music and beauty would flow. One who would think in terms like this, knew that sometimes a hand must be both firm and inviting simultaneously.

Her inspiration had struck her one rainy night when he had come over to show his latest lack of practice and dedication. He had demonstrated a complete lack of progress as the metronome clicked away the time. She walked around him, like an animal about to pounce, thinking of how to draw blood from this seeming stone. It had come like the lightning that played outside.

She began to yell. All the rage of wasted months poured forth as she berated him endlessly. Her eyes were aflame with the rage of cruel lands in the East. His impetuousness faded as it often does at its first challenge. He began to shrink. To cower. To sink in his own skin. Predictable. Then, once he was afraid of her, she did something that he had not at all expected. In a flash she slid her panties from under the skirt she was wearing. Her skirt remained down, concealing, but he could not help but imagine what it covered and what was uncovered. His eyes grew large both in anticipation of what may come and the fear that it was a dream he might wake from.

She walked towards him. Told him to stand up. He obeyed. She slapped him. Hard. He winced and stood mute. Shocked. A dream it was not. She grabbed hold of his hair and dragged him to the chair in the corner of the room. She forced him to his knees in front of her as she sat down, her legs wide in front of him. Terror had struck him and he remained mute.

"Now lick."

She forced his head, by the tuft of his hair to comply with her will.

He did.

He licked as she moved his head up and down to suit her desire. He tried to talk. She pulled his head back and struck him again, harder. A red handprint was left burned into his cheek.

"Just lick."

He said nothing after that..

She used him and moved his head. He was her instrument now and she played him with her eyes closed and her head back as her raven black hair cascaded over the back of the chair. She moved him to her purpose and she could feel his neck muscles relax and submit to her lead. Pleasure built and peaked. She cried out and pressed his face into her. He relented. He accepted her will over his own.

When she had finished she pushed him away onto the floor and lit a cigarette. He stared at her, unsure of what had happened, unsure of what was to come.

She looked at him, with dominant, piercing eyes and said, "This time, it was a punishment. Next time, it will be a reward, for working at your music – if I believe you are getting better. Do we have a deal?"

He nodded, his silent, shocked assent.

35.

Tarp

The house was a typical ranch. One floor, located in the middle of a sea of suburbs. Nothing special about it form the outside. But it wasn't a home. It was a warehouse.

I knocked on the front door with $30,000 in cash in a black

canvas bag slung over my shoulder. Capital for meth. A large buy. An expanding, growing business.

A man answered the door without saying a word. He knew me. I'd been there before. He waved me in. I entered and walked through the entry and took a left at the hall to the large, sunken floor living room. Business as usual.

I stopped short when I got there. Usually the man at the door was alone, but here on the sectional sat two other men. They were armed. This wasn't normal. Then, to my panic, my eyes sank down to the large blue tarp that covered the sunken part of the room. Tarps were definitely not fucking normal and my heart began to fibrillate. I knew they could see me sweating before the first drop of panic sweat ran down my face.

"I gotta piss." was all I could stammer as I rushed, headlong from the room.

I felt tears of panic welling in my eyes.

I went with the bag to the bathroom I knew was at the other end of the hall before anyone could say anything. I locked myself in, little good a hollow door would do to a murderous, malevolent, crazed drug dealer with rage and a machine gun, but it was all I could think of. My eyes darted around the small bathroom looking for options. No window. Just walls. No way out. I shouldn't have smoked this morning. Paranoia was cresting in me just at the time these men were going to kill me. I was terrified beyond words.

I had to get out. I had to get out of there or these men were going to kill me. Fight or flight time. No room for flight. All I could do was fight. I had no gun. I had no weapons. Just me and stupid bag of worthless fucking money. Shit. All I could think was that I should have listened to my fucking mother and stayed in school. That chain smoking bitch had been right.

I had to run. I couldn't fight. I had to make a mad dash from the windowless bathroom to the door. I knew the way. My heart was pounding and my blood thickened with copious amounts of excess adrenaline.

I opened the door and bolted for the front, screaming like a berserker through a haze of acrid cigarette smoke. No one could stop me. I was crazed. I was mad. I was desperate. I held the black canvas bag tightly to my side, held my head low and bowled down the hall.

I never even saw the iron fist that laid me low. It came from nowhere, from a calm head and a strong arm. I crumpled into a dazed pile on the floor. I started to cry, sobbing like a little girl would if you tipped over her tea party. The berserk was gone, all that was left was the lamentable, pitiful fear of being buried in a shallow hole somewhere nearby.

I looked up, through swollen moist eyes to see the confused, bearded face of a small but determined man. He was pointing a gun at me. I blubbered. I pleaded. I didn't want to die.

"What the fuck was all that?!" He demanded "I thought you were fucking cool!"

"I saw the tarp. I don't want to die. Please don't kill me..." I begged pathetically, snot running from my nose into my mouth.

"That's to trim the weed. We're waiting for delivery. We're not going to kill you stupid."

My heart slowed. A cool wave of relief ran up my body to my swollen, puffy eyes.

"Oh. OK". I said, wiping my nose on my sleeve.

We did our deal. I left still sniffling and I heard a roar of laughter as soon as the door clicked. I was sure it was at my expense. But in the end, it was only my pride and reputation that was hurt.

36.

Alley Murder

He didn't see me coming at first. He must have heard my footsteps in the snow, crushing as I ran towards him at full pace. He spun around. He hadn't seen me, but he'd been expecting trouble for days now. His body jerked around automatically and he threw up his hands to shield himself. It was too little, too late.

I outweighed him by fifty pounds and the momentum of my frame lifted him off his feet and slammed his body into the worn brick wall that lined the alley. His arms flew wildly at me, reaching for my face, but they missed the real danger of the drawn knife clenched in my hands. By the time he perceived the real danger, it was too late.

The momentum that had lifted him up was behind the knife blade too and it plunged into his belly. He cried out in pain as it did and I braced my left forearm over his mouth. It wouldn't be long now. Life would flow out of him from the savage wound he'd suffered, but there was life in him still. There was enough to cause harm or for him to lash out in some desperate, final act of revenge. Animals are at their most dangerous as the life is running out of them and men are no different. I pressed with my left forearm against his face. I pinned him to that wall, waiting for the end, as his body drained into the snow.

I was right to be cautious. Somewhere in this dying man a rage was unleashed and he railed against his attacker. His arms flailed. They punched. He scratched at my eyes and tried vainly to wrap his own hands around my neck as the blood pooled beneath our feet in the dirty snow. As it did, the snow absorbed it. First it was black, then red, and finally pink to white. A macabre fade in the snow between the feet of a killer and the not quite dead.

I pressed harder against his face and pulled the knife out. His skull was pinned against that wall, his eyes covered by my arm, but his hands still attacked blindly and without fear. Again, the knife struck out into this dying man's body. Again. My hand, sticky, slippery with this man's essence kept striking forward. The end hadn't come fast enough and I was eager to be done with this, eager for this man to pass. In the back of my mind, I wondered if he too was eager for this to be over. There was no way out now, but he had to fight. He had to fight against the end like we all will and do. But, I wondered again if part of him was just in a hurry to get it over with like I was. I stabbed. I stabbed. I stabbed.

His arms moved less. They moved with less vigor. The attacks became less intense. I knew it was happening. I knew he was growing sleepy. He was growing weaker. Cold was spreading through his body. Death would soon follow. I hoped it would for his sake. I hadn't meant for it to go on as long as it had. If it was all the same, I prefer it to be quick.

His arms fell to his side. Still.

It was over. Thank God. He was dead. I was done. I pulled the knife out and threw it to the blood soaked, snowy ground. All of his life had pooled at our feet. I lowered him down. Gently, with care. I sat him down, against that worn brick wall. His empty eyes looked at me vacantly. I closed them. Part from respect, and part from guilt. He didn't need to see anything now.

37.

Celebrity

The large, white, windowless van rolled down the winding dirt trail throwing up an enveloping cloud of dust in its wake. William was driving, he was the only person in the van, but he wasn't alone. His former employer lay dead in the back.

He had been a celebrity. He had been larger than life and hunted by an audience who could never get enough of him. His work was popular in the beginning. The money it had earned him had been more than enough to allow for the caprices of ten madmen in ten lifetimes, but it had never bought him what he had wanted. He had wanted peace. He had wanted to get away from it all, to be anonymous again and to live a quiet, private life with only those whom he had invited to share it with him. It had all eluded him.

His world, towards the end had become more and more public when all he had wanted was the opposite. People in the hospital sold the secret of his illness. They sold pictures too as he anguished and died a little more each day. It was plastered across the front pages of newspapers around the world before he had even heard the prognosis from his doctors. Money can buy a lot and well placed funds can break any confidentiality. His privacy had been broken and it had robbed him of his dying dignity.

It wasn't the end. The news had hit the media machine like the scent of blood to a school of starving sharks. The surged at him in a maddening fury, all trying to be the ones that could get the big scoop, the most shocking details about this man and his life, regardless of his wishes. He had become something to be used up, consumed. He wasn't a man with fears like them, he was a thing that they used to pay their bills. Greed drove them.

He had fled, he had tried to find refuge, somewhere, anywhere, but he had failed. Fans pursued him and alerted everyone to when they saw him. There was no privacy, anywhere in the world for this sick, old, scared, dying man. In the end, moments after he died, there was a bidding war for the first sad photos of his lifeless face. His body wasn't cold, but the bidding was heated. The world needed to savor this last taste of his all but used up corpse.

He had known this would come to pass. He was sick, but his mind was still as sharp as it'd ever been. He knew what would come afterward for his corpse. He knew it would find no rest. No peace would be offered to it. His resting place, anywhere in the world would become an unwelcome shrine, holding a body that wanted nothing more than to be forgotten. He had resolved to avoid this fate in death, even if he could not in life.

He set the millions in his treasury to buy, in death, that

what alluded him in life – peace. Attorneys were called in. Shell corporations formed. A patchwork of international red tape and subterfuge was created that would baffle even the most steadfast investigator. His money could not go with him and he turned every penny, pence, euro, yen and yuan he had to his end of finding peace – a final, lasting peace. In death, still, all he wanted was to be forgotten and to go unnoticed.

All that money, all that work, had been expended to buy the tract of land that held the dusty dirt road across which his lifeless body traveled in the windowless, white van. It was nowhere, it was empty, it was silent. The vast expanse would be his secret, peaceful tomb. No marker was to be raised. He had one already, in a cemetery back home. It had been widely publicized. The funeral had been large and public. Traffic had been stopped, a city had been gridlocked, all to bury an empty box. That empty box in the ground had turned into a shrine by obsessive, unwelcome fans who snapped pictures of themselves next to the headstone - a less than reverent practice.

Now, with faithful, loyal William driving him to his final resting place, he was sure of peace and secrecy.

William did his duty well and buried his former master, by

hand, without ceremony in the vast expanse. The lawyers might have secretly known about the thousands of acres, but only William knew the exact spot and would take it to his grave.

That would be sooner than William suspected. William was a good man, but his master had known, only too well, how greed and money turned good men wicked, especially when they carried a venal secret. The man who wanted to be forgotten had known that only too well. That's why a man was waiting to kill William before he could sell what he knew or pass the secret on.

It had worked for Alaric all those years ago when he had executed the men who'd buried him. His tomb, if not his name had been lost and forgotten. Plus, the dead men both believed that servants should not long outlive their masters.

38.

Charity

Nicholas led the man into the darkened cellar. He was only too happy to follow. The streets of the city were choked with soldiers deserting from the front. All the prime stoops were taken by others and gangs could be more of a threat to a lone man than the cold. The sun had fallen and an icy night blanketed the city. This man had to choose to either face the cold, alone and hungry or walk down into the dark, warm cellar after Nicholas' invitation. It was an easy choice to make.

This wasn't the first man, ravaged by war and forgotten by society, to whom Nicholas had offered hospitality. He was, after all a Christian and these men had suffered terribly. They had been the pride of the empire when they were facing bullets in the muddy trenches, but now, all that was over. They were no longer needed and those who were not one of them preferred to ignore them. They were a burden now on a country whose back already bent under too heavy a load. Many went hungry every night. More mouths to feed were an unwelcome burden most could not afford. None had time for charity, except Nicholas.

Nicholas showed the man to his bedding and even provided him with a small oil lamp to light the cellar. It was going to be cold, but warmer than outside and the man's greatcoat should keep him warm enough. At least on the straw in the cellar he would be safe from robbers, the cold and the rats.

The man thanked Nicholas profusely in the accent of an Eastern provincial. He was far from home and was overjoyed to find some kindness still existing in the cold world. Nicholas told him he would bring him some soup that he had cooked upstairs so he could eat before he slept. They both knew he was tired. There was no secret in that. There was a small table in the middle of the cellar with a small bench that he could eat at.

Again, the man thanked Nicholas in a torrent of praise for his Christian hospitality. After all, that which you do to the least of men, that you do unto Him.

Nicholas went upstairs and the man could hear him walking around, through the creaky, dusty floorboards over his head. Nicholas crossed back and soon his footsteps echoed down the worn wood cellar stairs. Good as his word, he had a steaming bowl in his hands. The man had not smelled fresh soup in longer than he could remember. It smelled just like his mother's cooking back home in the village. His stomach rumbled in eagerness for the repast.

He sat down at the table. Nicholas put the bowl in front of him and let the man eat. The clink of the spoon against the bowl as the man eagerly devoured the welcome food tapped out a chaotic melody. Nicholas knew he was hungry and let him eat without interrupting.

"Oh my. Your lamp is too close to the straw. That could

cause a fire." Nicholas rose and walked to the corner of the cellar to move the lamp.

The man kept slurping at the welcome hot soup. He had little mind for anything else.

Explosively, a cord pulled tight around the man's neck and a practiced, strong knee drove into his ribs forcing him to the table. The man's hands clawed instinctively, automatically at the garrote. He'd fought for his life and won many times in recent years, now was no different. He struggled, fought with a fury as he desperately grasped at the noose. Blood leaked from the claw marks his uncut, dirty nails left in his own neck as he frantically tried to loosen the taught rope. His eyes rolled back. His blood stopped. He fell, headfirst to the table his arms dangling lifelessly by his bent knees.

Nicholas undid the rope and walked up the stairs. He planned to deal with the man later. There was time and the soup would grow cold before long. He knew what to do. Above the cellar was a small butcher's storefront. No one ever asked where he got the sausages. They just paid and took them gratefully. Many were too hungry to wonder about such things. Tomorrow Nicholas' sausages would be fresh and he was certain he'd have a line.

I'm Falling In Love With You

Why the fuck does he think I like when he slaps my ass? That fucking hurts. I'm into it. I'm face down, ass up and he's pumping away. A girl needs a good fuck every now and again and then...smack. That fucking hurts. I bet I've got a hand print back there. Prick. Why do they all think that we're into that?

Well at least he hasn't tried to stick it in my ass yet. God, the last one just wouldn't take a hint. Kept "slipping". Oops. Sorry. Well, while we're here. Yeah, like I'm going to fall for that. You slipped and then I can't shit right for a couple of days. Yeah. No problem. You're cute so just jam it anywhere. God, where do they all get the idea that every girl is just going to start cumming as soon as they slip it into her ass. Yay! It's in my butt. That feels great. No. I'm being sarcastic.

What the fuck is he doing back there? How much longer is this going to take. I think at this point, I just want to be done. I'll tell him I have a meeting tomorrow, he'll be relieved and he'll go and then I can masturbate in the shower. I think that would be more fun. Maybe I'll call him around Christmas if I need a date. Damn, I don't want to go to my parents solo again. Is it worth it to let this ass slapper fuck me badly a few more times just so I have someone to go to Christmas dinner? It might be. Somehow, that seems wrong but it would shut my mother up for a few months. Bad sex is better than her emails and all her painful matchmaking. Oh, you know what so and so is up to these days...he's very successful you know...STOP! Just save it. I don't care.

Uggh. I don't even really like this guy anymore. I thought I did, but he's arrogant. Yeah he's cute, but this is getting old. Who's your daddy? Did he really just fucking say that? Now I think he's stupid. If I ever said "Who's your mommy?" to some guy I was riding his face would pucker in horror. But again, thank you porn, all these idiot guys think I want to be in bed with someone who is going to call themselves "my daddy". Lemme tell you, that is the last thing I want to think about while you are fucking me. Hey dad, while you're back there make sure to give it to me real good, I've been a naughty, little girl. Yuck! Please....

Why isn't he done yet? I'm not even wet anymore. Hey....Casanova, thanks for not noticing. Why am I not wet? Well, because Freddy Forget Foreplay just jammed it in like some drunken frat boy. Yeah genius, I am so turned

135

on by just being near you that I have to periodically ring out my panties. Yeah, that must be it. Nope. Still sarcastic. I've got to get down on my knees on my hardwood floors to suck your cock or it's nothing but a windsock, but you on the other hand just assume I'm always in a perfect state for you to mount and fuck forever. Yeah. That must be it.

Ugggh! Why isn't he done yet? Chaffing! It's like a submarine trying to swim through the Sahara.

This jackass better not pull out and cum all over me. I swear if one more guy does that, I'm going lesbian. Sure, I'm a little turned off by vagina but at least they won't cum all over my face and then look at me like I'm supposed to be really turned on instead of shocked and grossed out.

Wait! What was that? Did he just cum? There was a lot of grunting. Why is he still pumping? At least let me know what's going on. Group effort maybe? Courtesy anyone? Communicate!

OK. Finally. There it is. Yep, he's cumming. I know those stupid noises anywhere. Look at his face! Priceless! Best part of the date right there. OK good. Whew. Finally that's over with. OK. Time to get you out of here. I can't deal with you anymore tonight. You can go and my vibrator will tap in.

"That was incredible. You totally found my G-Spot baby. I think I'm falling in love with you."

There, that should send him running.

54534560R00083

Made in the USA
Middletown, DE
04 December 2017